CONTENTS

WELCOME BACK TO THE DREGS OF LAS VEGAS

VOLUME 3

This is a work of fiction. Names, characters, events, and incidents either are the product of the author's imagination or are used fictitiously. Any resemblance to actual persons, living or dead, or to real events is entirely coincidental.

ISBN: [979-8-9924766-5-1]

Published by Aaron Glassman

Printed in the United States of America

First Edition: [February, 2025]

This is story dedicated to all the loyal friends that had my back when it counted. There were only a few of you, don't everyone flatter yourselves.

also: Gratitude for the First Amendment

PROLOGUE

Welcome Back to the Dregs of Las Vegas

We return to the city that thrives on illusions—a place where glitz conceals grit. Behind the neon glow lies an underworld where survival means bending the rules or breaking them entirely. The dregs of this city don't dream of jackpots; they live off manipulations, schemes, and fleeting indulgences.

Here, morality is a gamble, loyalty is fleeting, and love? Just another transaction. For every high-roller basking in the limelight, there's someone in the shadows working an angle, turning desperation into currency.

This isn't the Vegas of glossy brochures. It's the residue of a city built on excess, deception, and the relentless pursuit of more. Welcome back to the Dregs of Las Vegas—a place where winning often costs more than you can afford to lose.

CHAPTER 1: COCO & THE CLERKS

Coco strutted into the department store like it was her personal runway, her heels clicking sharply against the polished marble floor. Heads turned as she moved, her dark hair cascading down her back in waves, her aura commanding attention without her needing to say a word. Her eyes, sharp and deliberate, scanned the racks with the precision of a predator sizing up its prey. She didn't check price tags or second-guess her selections; she simply plucked dresses, blouses, and jackets from their hangers with the ease of someone grabbing canned food off a grocery store shelf.

The rhythmic tapping of her heels paused near the jackets. Coco tossed her growing armful of garments onto a plush chair nearby, the pile spilling over like an overstuffed basket. A sales associate, a young woman with a practiced smile and neatly pinned hair, approached cautiously.

"Need any assistance today?" the clerk asked, her voice overly polite, almost hopeful.

"No, I'm good. Thanks," Coco replied, not even bothering to glance at her.

"Well, I can take those to the register for you while you shop," the clerk offered, her tone sweet but persistent.

Coco's eyes finally flicked to her, cool and dismissive. "No need.

I'm going to try these on," she said curtly, snatching the bundle of clothes from the clerk's hands.

The woman hesitated, her smile faltering. "Let me get you a dressing room," she tried again.

Coco's lips curled into a sharp smile, though there was no warmth in it. "I don't want your help," she snapped, her voice low and edged. "And when I check out, it won't be with you. Trust me on that." She walked away without waiting for a response, her heels clicking in an even tempo that signaled finality.

She headed straight to the men's section, where a young male clerk was arranging a display of neatly folded shirts. Coco waved him over with a flick of her wrist, her expression all business.

"I need you to try this on for my boyfriend," she said, holding up a green bomber jacket. Her tone was firm, authoritative. "You two are about the same size."

The clerk blinked, surprised but obliging. He was tall and wiry, with sleeves rolled up to his elbows, revealing toned forearms. "Of course," he said, slipping the jacket on as Coco appraised him with the intensity of a fashion editor.

"Yup, I like this," she said briskly. "Take it to the register—I'll buy it when I check out. Also, I need a dressing room."

He hesitated. "Wouldn't you be more comfortable in the women's dressing rooms?"

Coco's gaze sharpened, her lips curving into a sly smirk. "Nope. And unless you want to miss out on this sale, grab me a dressing room," she said, her tone a subtle challenge.

The clerk straightened, his professionalism winning out. "Right away, Miss."

Minutes later, Coco stood in the dressing room, the door purposefully left ajar by a crack. She peeled off her blouse, her large, perky breasts exposed to the cool, air-conditioned room, her nipples tightening in response. She adjusted her stance, angling herself so she could catch the clerk's eye through the sliver of open door.

When their gazes met, she beckoned him with a single crook of her finger, her expression teasing, daring. He froze for a moment, glancing over his shoulder as if expecting someone to intervene. When he turned back, she nodded, her lips curving into an inviting smile.

The clerk hesitated but took a step forward, then another, until he was inside the room with her. The door clicked softly shut behind him. Coco leaned against the wall, her pants already unbuttoned, slipping down her hips to reveal smooth skin and the absence of panties.

"I need a second opinion on these looks," she said, her voice dripping with mock innocence as she slipped on a Boho-style dress. The soft fabric clung to her curves. She turned to face him, her movements slow and deliberate. "What do you think?"

The clerk's throat worked as he swallowed hard, his cheeks flaming red. "Miss, it's against company policy to, um, be in the dressing rooms with customers," he stammered, his voice thick with nerves.

Coco leaned closer, her breath brushing against his ear. "Isn't the customer always right?" she whispered, her fingers trailing lightly over the front of his slacks.

His blush deepened, and he struggled to find his composure. "That dress... It looks, uh, very nice. It suits your complexion," he managed, his voice unsteady.

Coco tilted her head, her laughter low and throaty. She stepped back just enough to give him space, her gaze never leaving his face. "Good answer," she murmured, spinning in the dress for effect.

The tension in the air was electric, the room charged with Coco's undeniable control of the moment. She thrived on this—on teasing, luring, and leaving her marks breathless and off-kilter, tangled in her web of charm and audacity.

She pulled off the dress, bouncing around in her birthday suit, her ample breasts swaying with each movement.

"What do you think about this shirt?" she asked, grabbing a green graphic tee and slipping it on—still without any bottoms.

"I think you might wanna see how it looks with blue jeans," he replied nervously.

"What, you don't think it looks good like this?" she shot back, aggressively grabbing his bulge and breathing heavily in his face. Leaning in, she whispered, "Feel how wet my pussy is," her voice dripping with dominance as she bit his earlobe.

Before he could respond, she seized his hand, guiding it forcefully between her legs. She pressed his fingers against her shaved, rosy pink lips, already slick with arousal. He hesitated, but she pushed him further, and he began to probe lightly, tracing circles that made her gasp and close her eyes.

With one swift motion, her hands went to his belt, deftly unbuckling it. She unzipped his pants and pulled down his underwear, freeing a thick, veiny shaft with a bulbous head. Dropping to her knees, she inspected him with an intense, almost predatory gaze.

"This is just what I wanted to try on," she said, resting his heavy length against her face and locking eyes with him.

The clerk exhaled sharply, barely able to process what was happening. "I can't believe this is real," he muttered.

"Believe it, you dumb fuck—it's your lucky day," she snapped, her tone both mocking and commanding. She spat on his dick, rubbing her saliva all over it with meticulous strokes, repeating the action for good measure. Then, without warning, she stood, bent over, and teed up her dripping pussy and ass for him.

"Put it all in. Now," she demanded.

He didn't hesitate, gripping her hips and pressing his fat head into her warm, wet slit. She moaned as he plunged deeper, each thrust exploring a new angle inside her.

"Pull my hair," she ordered, and he obeyed, wrapping her locks around his hand as he thumped into her rhythmically. Her cheeks flushed, and her breathing grew ragged with each pounding stroke.

"Spit on my asshole," she commanded again, her voice edged with lust. He complied, watching as the spit dripped down, mixing with the slick fluids coating their fevered bodies.

"I can't hold it back anymore," he said, panting heavily as his thrusts became erratic.

"No! Don't cum yet. Don't you dare," she barked, pushing back against his glistening length. "Hold it."

"I can't—I'm gonna bust!" he exclaimed, pulling out at the last second.

She dropped to her knees, her mouth wide open, tongue out. "Don't let it go to waste. Put it in my mouth," she said, her voice like a purr.

Leaning against the dressing room wall, he took two shaky breaths, stroking himself as thick ropes of cum shot into her glossy, pouty lips. She swallowed it all without flinching, smirking as he collapsed into the chair behind him, spent and overwhelmed.

"Get off my clothes, you two-pump chump," she snarled, shoving him aside. "I didn't even get to cum, you eager-beaver fuck."

Grabbing her bundle of clothes, she shoved them into her bag.

The clerk, still disoriented, didn't even notice her stuffing every item from the dressing room into her bag. She shook her head, pulling on her clothes and shoes before sauntering out of the stall.

"Can I get your number or Instagram?" he called after her weakly, still trying to regain his composure.

"I know where to find you if I need you again," she said coolly, not breaking stride. Glancing back over her shoulder, she added, "Work on lasting longer, and there might be a next time, you fat-dick store clerk."

With that, she strutted out of the department store, several thousand dollars 'worth of stolen merchandise swinging in her bag, leaving the clerk spellbound and slack-jawed in the dressing room. The sharp click of her heels on the polished marble floor echoed her triumph, a brazen symphony of defiance that silenced even the distant chatter of unsuspecting shoppers. She tossed her hair over her shoulder, a sly smile curling her lips as the automatic doors slid open, ushering her into the sunlit chaos of the parking lot. Coco knew she'd left her mark, a whirlwind of audacity that the clerk would never forget—and likely never experience again.

As she disappeared into the rows of cars, a security guard glanced her way but hesitated, distracted by a distant call on his radio. Coco's confidence was her shield; she knew the world wasn't built to stop someone like her. She slipped into her car, tossing the bag onto the passenger seat, and lit a cigarette, savoring the taste of her victory. "Next time," she murmured to herself, exhaling a plume of smoke, "Shoes are on the list." With a smirk, she revved the engine, the tires squealing as she vanished into the horizon, leaving behind nothing but the scent of her body-lotion and the chaos she'd orchestrated.

CHAPTER 2: MEGAN'S FALSE FLAG

Megan lounged on the plush leather sofa in Brayden's high-rise condo, her perfectly manicured nails tapping against her phone screen. The view of the Las Vegas Strip sprawled before her, a neon-drenched dreamscape stretching into the late afternoon haze. She admired her reflection in the floor-to-ceiling windows —effortlessly stunning, as always. The sleek lines of her designer dress hugged her body just right, her makeup still flawless from earlier. She liked this life, the comfort, the ease. But it wasn't enough. It never was.

Brayden emerged from the bedroom, dressed in a sleek workout set, his water bottle in one hand, phone in the other. He barely looked at her as he adjusted the strap of his gym bag over his shoulder.

"I'm heading to the gym," he muttered, scrolling through his phone.

Megan glanced up, feigning disinterest. "Again? Didn't you just go yesterday?"

Brayden snorted. "Yeah, well, gotta keep up appearances." His tone dripped with sarcasm, but she caught the flicker of unease behind his expression.

"Don't work out too hard," she quipped with a smirk. The double meaning hung in the air between them.

Brayden shot her a look, his lips twitching into something like a smirk, but his eyes stayed unreadable. "Try not to start any drama while I'm gone."

She offered him a sickly sweet smile. "Who, me?"

The door clicked shut behind him. Megan exhaled sharply, rolling her eyes, and tapped into her contacts. Her finger hovered over a familiar name—Bradford. She hadn't called him in weeks, hadn't needed to. But she was bored. And she was pissed. And that was always a dangerous combination.

She hit the call button. The line rang. Once. Twice.

"What do you want, Megan?" Bradford's voice was flat, uninterested.

She pouted, even though he couldn't see it. "Hi to you too, Brad. Missed me?"

A scoff. "Not in the slightest."

Megan leaned back into the couch, stretching out like a cat in a sunbeam. "You don't have to pretend, you know. We had something, and—"

"What we had was you lying to my face about being pregnant," Bradford cut her off, his voice sharper now, the edge she had been looking for. "And for what, Megan? To see how I'd react? To manipulate me into giving a shit? You're fucking insane."

"Oh, come on," she sighed, twisting a strand of hair around her finger. "It wasn't *that* bad."

"That bad?" he snapped. "You faked a goddamn pregnancy while still playing house with Brayden. And you expect me to just what? Get over it? Pretend it didn't happen?"

"I was desperate, Brad," she said, her voice turning softer, laced with faux vulnerability. "I just... I needed to know if you really cared."

Bradford let out a bitter laugh, the kind that wasn't amused at all. "You needed to know if I cared, so you lied about carrying my kid? Megan, that isn't desperation. That's fucking *sociopathic*."

Her jaw tightened. "Don't be so dramatic."

"Dramatic?" Bradford's voice turned icy. "You *are* the drama, Megan. You create chaos and then pretend to be the victim when it all blows up in your face."

Megan clenched her phone. "You didn't even let me explain—"

"There's nothing to explain! You're a liar, Megan. A manipulative, self-absorbed liar. And for what? To keep my attention? Newsflash: *You lost it.*"

She felt the sting of his words more than she wanted to admit. "You're overreacting," she muttered, but the usual venom in her voice faltered.

"No, I'm finally reacting the way I *should have* from the start," he shot back. "We're done. Lose my number."

The line went dead before she could say another word. Megan stared at the screen, anger bubbling beneath the surface. How *dare* he talk to her like that? Like she was disposable. Like she wasn't *worth* the chaos she created.

"Asshole," she muttered under her breath, tossing her phone onto the couch.

The sound of the elevator dinging snapped her back to reality. Brayden strolled in, his gym bag slung over his shoulder, a smoothie in his hand. He took one look at her and raised an eyebrow. "You look like you just got chewed up and spit out."

Megan straightened, forcing a smile. "Just stupid girl drama."

Brayden smirked knowingly. "Kimber?"

"None of your business." She stood, brushing past him toward the kitchen.

Brayden chuckled, shaking his head. "You know, you might want to lay off the theatrics, Megan. One day, it's all going to blow up in your face."

She stopped mid-step, turning to glare at him. "Thanks for the unsolicited advice, Dr. Phil."

"Anytime." He popped the cap on his smoothie and took a sip, watching her with a mix of amusement and wariness.

Megan poured herself a glass of wine, staring out at the neon-lit Strip. The city glowed like a siren, calling to the desperate and the depraved, its flashing billboards and pulsing energy masking the rot beneath. She took a slow sip, letting the warmth settle in her chest, but it did nothing to quiet the gnawing unease twisting in her gut.

She had everything she thought she wanted—an upscale condo with a view, designer bags stacked in the closet, a man who kept up appearances and never asked too many questions. From the outside, her life looked pristine, polished to perfection like the marble countertops in Brayden's kitchen. But beneath the surface, cracks were already forming. The lies she told—about Bradford, about the pregnancy, about everything—were starting to overlap, tangling into a mess she was losing control of.

Brayden wasn't stupid. He played along because it benefited him, but there was a limit to how much bullshit even he would tolerate. And Bradford—he was different. He was the one thing she couldn't manipulate the way she wanted. His rejection tonight stung more than she'd admit, not because she loved him, but because she hated losing control.

She glanced at her phone, half-expecting a message from Bradford, some last-minute change of heart, but the screen stayed dark. He was really done. For now.

The thought sent a surge of defiance through her. She'd been in tighter spots before. People didn't just walk away from her. Not for long. She would fix this. She always did.

Outside, the Strip hummed with life, a city built on illusion and reinvention. Megan smirked to herself, swirling the wine in her glass. One day, everything might come crashing down. The lies, the deception, the carefully constructed house of cards she called a life.

But not today.

CHAPTER 3: TAMMY'S REVENGE

The dim, neon glow of Dino's Dive Bar was a sharp contrast to the blistering Vegas heat outside. Tammy perched on a barstool, her long legs crossed and her perfectly manicured nails tapping against a half-empty glass of whiskey. Her tousled blonde hair framed her face, but her bloodshot eyes hinted at the night she was trying to drink away. She scanned the room with a practiced nonchalance until her gaze landed on Bradford, leaning casually against the far end of the bar.

"Well, well, if it isn't Mr. DJ," Tammy said, sliding off her stool and strutting toward him with a sultry sway in her hips.

Bradford, mid-sip of his beer, glanced up and let out a low sigh. "Tammy. Didn't expect to see you here."

"Funny, I could say the same," Tammy purred, sidling up next to him. "What's it been, Brad? A year? Two?"

"Not long enough," Bradford muttered under his breath, taking another sip.

Tammy ignored the jab, leaning in closer. "You look good. Better than I remember. What brings you to this fine establishment? Slumming it for old time's sake?"

"Just grabbing a drink," Bradford replied, his tone curt. "And before you ask, no, I'm not interested in whatever game you're trying to play."

Tammy feigned a pout, her fingers tracing the rim of her glass. "Game? Can't a girl catch up with an old friend?"

Bradford turned to face her, his eyes narrowing. "You're not here to catch up, Tammy. You never are. So why don't you cut the crap and tell me what you want?"

Tammy smirked, her lips curving into a dangerous smile. "Fine. I heard Tiffany's back in town. That true?"

Bradford's jaw tightened. "Why does it matter?"

"Oh, come on," Tammy said, rolling her eyes. "Don't act like you don't know. That bitch fucking electrocuted me. I just want to make sure she's not getting too comfortable."

Bradford shook his head, exhaling sharply. "You're unbelievable. Yeah, she's back. She's with some MMA guy now. Westin something. Met him at the gym the other day."

Tammy's eyes gleamed with interest. "Westin Wexford?"

"Yeah, that's the one," Bradford replied, already regretting saying anything.

Tammy leaned in, her hand resting on his arm. "Thanks for the tip. I owe you one."

Bradford pulled away, his expression hardening. "You don't owe me anything, Tammy. And whatever you're planning, leave me out of it."

"Suit yourself," Tammy said with a wink, tossing back the rest of her drink. "But you're missing out."

Bradford watched her saunter away, shaking his head. "Trashiest bitch I've ever met," he muttered under his breath, turning back to his beer.

Pitbull Iron Works Gym – The Next Day

The pounding bass of the gym's speakers throbbed against Tammy's eardrums, each beat ricocheting through her hungover haze. Pitbull Iron Works wasn't a glamorous, high-end fitness center; it was gritty and raw—the walls scuffed from heavy lifting, the faint smell of rubber mats and sweat permeating the air. Fluorescent lights hummed overhead, reflecting off dusty mirrors and rows of iron plates. Tammy's oversized sunglasses did little to shield her from the harsh glare, but she wore them anyway, a small barrier between her and the world.

She spotted Westin Wexford easily across the gym. He stood taller than the other patrons, his broad shoulders and sculpted arms making him a focal point among the usual crowd of grunting lifters. As he bobbed and weaved in front of a mirror, shadowboxing with laser focus, his muscles rippled beneath a thin layer of sweat. Tammy felt her pulse quicken. Even through her lingering headache, she couldn't deny the spark of anticipation that danced along her skin.

Sliding her sunglasses to the top of her head, Tammy sauntered over. Her tight workout leggings clung to her legs and hips, and her cropped tank top exposed the slight sheen of perspiration on her stomach. She didn't bother hiding the appraising glance she gave him—she wanted him to notice.

"Westin, right?" Her voice came out in a sweet, breathy lilt.

He turned, narrowing his eyes. "Yeah. Who's asking?"

"Tammy," she replied, offering a brilliant smile that briefly masked her hangover. She took in the sculpted curve of his jaw and the faint lines of tension around his eyes—signs of a fighter's discipline. "I've seen you fight. You're impressive."

A flicker of pride crossed Westin's face. "Thanks. You train here?"

She shook her head, letting her hair tumble. "First time," she lied smoothly. "Figured I'd check it out. You mind showing me around?"

Westin paused, as though sizing her up, then shrugged. "Sure. Follow me."

Tammy trailed him through the maze of weight racks, treadmills, and punching bags, nodding politely at his short explanations—though her gaze kept drifting to the flex of his back and shoulders. Eventually, they reached a door with a small sign reading "Steam Room." Thick clouds of moisture wafted out each time it opened.

"Oh, co-ed," Tammy observed with a tilt of her head. "Mind if I join you in there?"

Without waiting for an answer, her fingertips lightly grazed the outside of his gym shorts—enough to send a ripple of awareness up his spine. Westin raised an eyebrow, half-curious, half-wary, but didn't stop her. She pushed the door open, and a wave of hot, moist air rolled over them.

Inside the Steam Room

The steam room was a dim, tiled chamber awash in swirling clouds of heat. Soft overhead lighting created a hazy glow, casting blurred shadows against the walls. The humidity clung to every surface; even the bench along the wall seemed to glisten with condensation. Each breath Tammy took felt dense with moisture and the faint scent of eucalyptus or menthol lingering in the air.

Tammy's skin immediately prickled under the enveloping warmth. Her clothes felt heavier—clinging to her body, saturated in seconds. She slipped out of her tank top and leggings with smooth efficiency, letting them drop onto a wooden shelf near the door. Droplets formed on her bare shoulders and arms, rolling down her torso in shimmery trails. Westin, taller and broader, loomed over her like a statue carved from muscle—his expression a mixture of intrigue and hesitation. But he didn't protest as she pressed close.

Her hands drifted over the ridges of his abdomen, and she felt the tension in his body as he inhaled sharply. The steam coiled around them, intensifying the heat that pulsated between their bodies. Tammy leaned up, lips grazing the shell of his ear. The heat of her breath mingled with the damp air.

"Relax," she murmured, voice husky with intent. "You deserve a break."

Westin's gaze flicked downward as if weighing the risk, then he exhaled in a slow, measured breath. Tammy could practically feel the moment his resistance melted away. The tension in his broad shoulders softened as she pressed her chest against him, the slickness of their skin creating a charged friction. Each subtle movement became magnified: the soft slide of her thigh against his, the press of his palm at the small of her back.

Their shared breath mixed with the swirling steam, and droplets formed on Westin's dark lashes. Tammy wound her arms around his neck, pulling him down for a slow, burning kiss that left no room for second-guessing. The taste of salt from sweat lingered on her lips, and she felt the resonance of his low groan in her own chest.

Time warped in the heated haze. The constant hiss of steam drowned out the clank of weights and the distant hum of the gym's speakers. Every sense honed in on the slick glide of their bodies, the steamy pressure hugging them, the rapid thud of her heartbeat echoing in her ears. Tammy's breath hitched when Westin's hands traced her curves with a fighter's control—strong yet deliberate. The tiny tile patterns on the bench pressed into her skin when he momentarily backed her against it, water droplets cooling against her hot flesh.

Every so often, Tammy caught a glimpse of her bag near the doorway, its contents hidden. She remembered the phone quietly recording, capturing each gasp and whispered word. But in the moment, her focus remained on the primal tension crackling between them—on Westin's steady grip at her hip, the warm press of his lips against her collarbone, and the humid swirl enveloping them like a secret, steamy cocoon.

Their voices dissolved into breathy murmurs and the soft echo of contact on damp tile. There was an edge of the forbidden here—an unspoken realization that they were in a public place, that at any second someone might open the door. That risk underpinned the wild thrum of adrenaline coursing through both of them.

Eventually, they sank onto the bench, bodies still entwined. Tammy's pulse hammered so loudly she couldn't distinguish it from the bass in the gym outside. She blinked, sweat and condensation dripping from her lashes, and found Westin watching her with hooded eyes. His breath came in short, ragged intervals, his shoulders rising and falling. In that charged, humid bubble, she couldn't decide which was hotter—the steam suffocating the space or the electricity strung between them.

She gave him a small, provocative smile as she brushed a hand over his cheek, collecting a bead of sweat with her fingertip. He swallowed hard, and for a second, Tammy glimpsed the fighter's discipline lurking beneath his desire. She wondered how he'd react when he learned of her hidden motive—if he'd suspect, if he'd ever know. But she pushed the thought away, letting the tension linger as the steam swirled around them, sealing them in temporary oblivion.

Outside, the gym remained unaware—just a few feet and a heavy door away. Inside, the air was thick with promise and the tang of salt, skin, and possibility. Tammy leaned in, her lips brushing his ear once more.

"You'll thank me later," she whispered, though whether she meant for this fleeting escape or for something else entirely, even she wasn't certain.

Westin's only response was a deep exhale, his chest rumbling against hers. And for now, that was enough.

Later That Evening

Sitting in the driver's seat with the engine idling, Tammy rewatched the steamy footage on her phone, letting it play in slow motion. Each frame of Westin's betrayal sent a rush of satisfaction through her veins—a potent cocktail of triumph, anger, and exhilaration. The gym's neon sign flickered ominously on the periphery, and she couldn't help but think how fitting it was: the neon against the darkness, just as her intentions shone against the shadow of her own bitterness.

The memory of Dino's dive bar flashed in her mind. She could still feel the sting of that night—both literal and figurative. Dino's, with its flickering overhead lights and sticky floors, had been the backdrop for the worst humiliation of her life. Tiffany, strutting around like she owned the place, had lured Tammy into a confrontation. And then came the taser: a sharp, electrifying pain that locked her muscles and sent her sprawling. The shock itself lasted only seconds, but the mortification lingered for years.

Tammy still heard the echoes of laughter from onlookers who did nothing but stand by and watch her convulse on the floor. She remembered Tiffany's triumphant smirk as she held that taser just a fraction of an inch too close. That night had turned Tammy's stomach for weeks—no, months—every time she thought of it. Even now, she could feel the phantom ache where the metal prongs had made contact, forever branding her with a sense of rage and retribution.

She dragged her gaze back to the phone screen. There it was— hot, heavy evidence of Westin Wexford letting himself get caught in Tammy's trap. If Tiffany thought she could go through life unscathed after inflicting that humiliation, she had another thing coming.

"Revenge," Tammy mouthed silently, tasting the word. It felt good on her tongue, like a shot of something strong and burning. She tapped a few times on her phone, unblocking Tiffany's number with a cool sense of finality. The old messages scrolled up— taunts, threats, half-finished pleas. All water under the bridge now. Tammy smirked as she attached the incriminating video, her heart pounding with glee at the thought of Tiffany's reaction.

Tammy: *Thought you'd want to know what your boyfriend's been up to. Enjoy.*

It took only a second for the video to load, then a blink of an eye for it to send. A confirmation beep followed—a delicious little note that made Tammy's skin prickle with anticipation. She pictured Tiffany's shock, her devastation, the way her carefully curated world would come crashing down the moment she pressed play.

It wasn't just about catching Tiffany off guard. It was about ripping away Tiffany's security, showing her that she wasn't the only one who could wield power. Tammy thought of the nights she'd tossed and turned, replaying that taser incident again and again—wishing she'd had the upper hand, a weapon of her own. This video was that weapon: an emotional taser that would leave Tiffany writhing with betrayal and heartbreak.

She stared at the flickering reflection of headlights in the rearview mirror, the bright illusions of the Vegas Strip dancing just beyond. It was almost poetic—this city of illusions, where neon glitz masked every heartbreak and scandal, was exactly the stage Tammy needed to enact her revenge.

The glow of her phone illuminated her face in sharp contrast, highlighting the slight curl of her lip and the unmistakable malice in her eyes. She pictured Tiffany, phone in hand, her confident smirk vanishing into shock. Tammy wanted her to feel exposed, humiliated—just like she'd been at Dino's. She wanted Tiffany to know that some wounds never truly healed, and that a single spark of hate could ignite a wildfire of vengeance, even after years.

As the text officially marked "delivered," Tammy let her imagination run wild. Maybe Tiffany would break down crying. Maybe she'd confront Westin in a rage, tossing his clothes onto the street. Maybe she'd come after Tammy, screaming and swearing. The specifics didn't matter—all that mattered was the devastation. She wanted Tiffany to feel the slow, creeping dread that Tammy had endured after that night at Dino's, when she couldn't sleep without replaying the humiliation over and over in her mind.

She nudged her phone onto the passenger seat, her pulse still thrumming with excitement. Deep down, Tammy knew this wouldn't erase the past. She knew no act of revenge, no matter how perfectly orchestrated, could truly reverse time or erase that searing sting of a taser. But the knowledge that Tiffany would now taste a similar kind of helplessness gave her a dark sense of satisfaction—an intoxicating sense of justice served cold.

The engine revved under her foot as she pulled away from the curb. Outside, the fluorescent gym lights and gaudy neon of the city spun into streaks of color in her rearview mirror. Each turn of the wheel felt like a step deeper into the shadowy corners of her own soul—corners she hadn't realized existed until Dino's turned her life upside down.

"She thought she could just... walk away," Tammy muttered to herself, lips twisting. The memory of Tiffany's smug laughter replayed like a broken record. "Not this time."

The city's shimmering horizon stretched before her, beckoning in its usual desert allure. But this time, the city lights weren't just decorations; they were footnotes to Tammy's personal vendetta, a labyrinth of possibilities in which she could toy with Tiffany's life. And if Tiffany dared come after her? Good. Tammy was finished playing the victim. She had her ammunition now—literal footage of Tiffany's man hooking up with someone else. It was the ultimate payback, sweetened by the knowledge that Tiffany's little world would never be the same.

An exultant shiver ran through Tammy as she let the adrenaline settle. She turned on the radio, letting the throbbing beats guide her out onto the open road. Tomorrow, there would be fresh drama—new messages, furious calls, maybe even a tearful confrontation in a parking lot somewhere. She welcomed it. After all, Tiffany had lit this fire the moment she pressed that taser against Tammy's flesh. Now, Tammy was simply returning the favor in a far more calculated way.

With one final, self-satisfied glance at her phone, she accelerated into the night, leaving behind the scene of her latest conquest. She felt the glow of neon pulsing like a second heartbeat—a testament to her newfound power and the havoc she intended to unleash. As she vanished into the Vegas streets, only one certainty remained: Tammy wasn't finished with Tiffany. Not by a long shot.

CHAPTER 4: VERONICA'S SHIFT

The dim glow of the neon lights filtering through Veronica's apartment windows cast an ethereal glow on the meticulously curated chaos of her living space. Designer clothes draped over chairs, high-end cameras on the coffee table, and stacks of Polaroids scattered across the floor painted a picture of her calculated, glamorous world. Veronica lounged on her velvet sofa, scrolling through her OnlyFans account, her polished red nails tapping against her phone screen.

The sudden buzz of the intercom jolted her out of her focus. She walked to the panel, her heels clicking on the hardwood floor, and pressed the button.

"It's me," Slim Mo's voice rasped through the speaker.

She sighed, a mix of irritation and resignation clouding her features. "Come up," she replied, buzzing him in.

Moments later, Slim Mo strolled into her apartment, his lanky frame draped in an oversized hoodie and a cloud of weed smoke clinging to him like a signature scent. His bleached hair stuck out in haphazard spikes, and his blue eyes scanned the room with casual disdain.

"Nice digs," he muttered, flopping onto the sofa uninvited.

"What do you want, Slim?" Veronica asked, her tone sharp but not hostile as she leaned against the doorframe, arms crossed.

Slim leaned back, spreading out like he owned the place. "We gotta talk about money, Vee. Those videos we made? They're blowing up, but all I see is chump change."

Veronica arched an eyebrow. "I already gave you a thousand, Slim. That's what we agreed on."

"Yeah, well, it's not enough," he said, his tone laced with irritation. "You're pulling in racks off my dick, and I'm out here scraping by. I want more."

She rolled her eyes, walking over to the counter where a sleek, metallic clutch lay. She pulled out a crisp stack of bills and tossed it onto the coffee table. "There's another five hundred. Take it or leave it."

Slim stared at the cash but made no move to grab it. Instead, he leaned forward, his expression shifting from irritated to something darker. "You know, we could make more if you stopped being so stuck-up. Why don't we film something new tonight? Just you and me."

Veronica's laugh was sharp and derisive. "You've got to be kidding me. That's not happening, Slim."

He shrugged, unfazed. "Come on, Vee. You used to love it. What's the big deal?"

She stepped closer, her gaze hard and unyielding. "The big deal is, I've moved on. I've got new talent lined up, and frankly, you're old news."

Slim's smirk faltered, replaced by a flash of anger. "Old news, huh? After everything I did for you, you're just gonna toss me aside like that?"

Veronica leaned in, her voice dropping to a venomous whisper.

"Don't get it twisted, Slim. You didn't do shit for me. I built this, not you. And just so we're clear, we're done—professionally and personally."

Slim stood abruptly, his lanky frame towering over her. "Fine, bitch. But don't come crying to me when your stash runs dry. You think your new dealer's gonna front you the good stuff?"

Veronica didn't flinch, her hand slipping into her clutch and pulling out a small, sleek revolver. She held it loosely at her side, her expression unchanging. "Let me make something clear, Slim. You're not my dealer anymore. You're not my anything. So get the hell out of my place."

Slim's eyes widened at the sight of the gun, but he quickly masked his surprise with a scoff. "You're crazy, you know that?"

"Maybe," she said with a cold smile. "But I'm also done with your bullshit. Door's that way."

For a moment, they stood in tense silence, the weight of her words hanging heavily in the air. Finally, Slim snatched the cash from the table, stuffing it into his hoodie pocket.

"You'll regret this, Vee," he said, backing toward the door.

"I doubt it," she replied, her voice icy.

With a final glare, Slim turned and left, slamming the door behind him. Veronica exhaled, setting the revolver back into her clutch and walking over to the window. She watched him disappear down the street, a sense of relief washing over her.

"This city's full of Slim Mo's," she muttered to herself, turning back to her phone. "Time to find someone who knows how to play the game."

She sat back on the couch, scrolling through profiles of potential new collaborators, her sharp green eyes gleaming with determination. Slim was just another chapter closed in her relentless climb to the top.

CHAPTER 5: KYLER BEHIND BARS

The sterile chill of the jail's visitor room clung to Brayden's skin like an unwelcome fog. The fluorescent lights overhead buzzed faintly, casting a pale, unflattering glow over the dingy gray walls. The room was divided by a thick, double-paned glass partition, smudged with fingerprints and the faint, greasy outlines of faces pressed too close in moments of desperation.

Brayden adjusted the lapel of his tailored gray suit, his polished appearance a sharp contrast to the oppressive bleakness of the room. Across the glass, Kyler sat in a bright orange jumpsuit that clung awkwardly to his lean frame. His sandy blond hair was disheveled, and his jawline was dusted with the beginnings of a beard. His piercing blue eyes, though weary, were defiant as they locked on Brayden's.

Brayden picked up the black plastic phone receiver on his side of the glass, motioning for Kyler to do the same. Kyler hesitated for a moment before lifting the receiver, his movements slow, deliberate.

"I'm Brayden O'Connor," Brayden began, his voice calm but firm. "Your sister Kimber hired me to take on your case."

Kyler leaned forward, his brow furrowing. "Yeah, she said she would. I called her, told her to get me someone good. So here you are. What's the deal, man?"

Brayden took a deep breath, his polished demeanor unwavering. "First things first—have you spoken to the police or anyone else about the charges against you?"

Kyler shook his head. "Hell no. I'm not stupid. I know better than to run my mouth."

"Good," Brayden said, nodding approvingly. "Let's go over the charges. You're looking at allegations of sexual assault and domestic assault and battery from Chloe Rivera. On top of that, your prior record isn't doing you any favors—possession charges for narcotics, two priors for assault. It's not a good look."

Kyler sat back in his chair, his expression darkening. "Chloe's full of shit," he spat. "She's making all this up. She's just mad because I kicked her out of my place. She's trying to ruin my life."

Brayden raised a hand, signaling for him to calm down. "Keep your voice down," he said evenly. "I need facts, not emotions. What happened the night you were arrested?"

Kyler exhaled sharply, his frustration palpable. "She showed up drunk, screaming about God knows what. We argued, yeah, but I didn't lay a hand on her. Next thing I know, the cops are at my door, and she's spinning some bullshit story."

Brayden tilted his head slightly, scrutinizing Kyler's expression. "Have you seen her toxicology report? Her bloodwork from that night?"

Kyler leaned forward, his voice lowering. "No, but you should. She was high as a kite, man. She's been on coke and pills for years. Look at her bloodwork. That'll prove she wasn't in her right mind."

Brayden tapped his fingers against the table, considering the angle. "I'll get the report, but let's be realistic, Kyler. Your record doesn't exactly scream 'innocent bystander. 'The prosecution's going to lean hard on that, and the jury won't look kindly on it."

Kyler's jaw tightened, his eyes blazing with determination. "I don't care what they lean on. I didn't do what she's saying I did, and I'm not taking some bullshit plea deal. You hear me? I'm not guilty."

Brayden sighed, his professional mask slipping just enough to reveal a flicker of frustration. "Listen, I'm on your side, but I have to tell you the truth. This isn't looking good for you. A plea deal might be your best option."

Kyler shook his head adamantly. "No way. I'm not pleading guilty to something I didn't do. You're my lawyer, right? So do your job. Get that toxicology report, dig up whatever you can, and prove she's lying."

Brayden studied him for a long moment, weighing his options. Finally, he nodded. "Alright. I'll look into it. But you need to keep your head down in here and stay out of trouble. The last thing we need is you making things worse for yourself."

Kyler smirked faintly, though there was no humor in it. "Don't worry about me, man. I can handle myself."

Brayden glanced at his watch, then back at Kyler. "I'll be in touch once I've got more information. In the meantime, sit tight."

Kyler leaned back, the faintest hint of relief flickering across his face. "Thanks, man."

Brayden hung up the receiver and stood, straightening his suit as he walked toward the exit. The heavy metal door clanged shut behind him, the sound echoing in the sterile hallway. As he left the jail, the weight of the case settled on his shoulders. Kyler was defiant, but defiance alone wouldn't win a courtroom battle. This was going to be a long, uphill fight.

CHAPTER 6: A HIGH-STAKES ARRANGEMENT

The first rays of dawn spilled over the Las Vegas Strip, cutting through the smoggy haze and spilling like liquid gold into Brittany's penthouse. Her lair—because that's what it felt like—was all gleaming surfaces and sharp lines, a study in excess. White marble floors stretched beneath oversized abstract paintings that screamed "expensive," while the glass coffee table was littered with the aftermath of last night: lipstick-smeared champagne flutes, an empty bottle of Dom, and a pair of sky-high Louboutins abandoned like casualties of war.

On the bed—a sprawling, custom-made monstrosity that could have comfortably slept six—Bradford lay sprawled, naked but for the rumpled sheets draped over his hips. His lean, sun-kissed body looked sculpted in the early light, the kind of physique that didn't come from hard work but from good genes and just enough gym selfies to keep up appearances. His dark hair stuck up in messy spikes, evidence of Brittany's fingers from hours earlier.

Brittany perched beside him, propped up on one elbow, her honey-blonde hair falling in loose waves over her shoulder. Her silk robe had slipped low, revealing the swell of her breast and a faint scar from her last enhancement. Her perfectly arched brows framed eyes the color of a poison-green cocktail, sharp and assessing even at this ungodly hour.

Bradford stirred, opening one eye lazily as his lips curled into a smirk. "Morning, boss," he drawled, his voice thick with sleep and leftover whiskey. "Or should I call you ma'am?"

She snorted softly, brushing a strand of hair from his forehead. "Call me whatever you want, baby. As long as you keep looking at me like that."

"Like what?" He yawned, stretching out with an infuriating amount of ease. "Like I'm a man who knows exactly how lucky he is to wake up in this bed?"

Her smile was catlike. "Something like that."

"Don't get used to it," he teased, though his tone lacked conviction. "I've got, you know, things to do. Places to be."

She chuckled, low and throaty, before leaning down, her lips grazing his ear. "Bradford, sweetie, the only place you need to be is exactly where I tell you."

The heat between them was electric, but it was a fire built on precarious kindling. Brittany wasn't just his sugar mama—she was a queen holding court, and Bradford was the latest court jester in her lineup of pretty boys.

"So," he said, sitting up and reaching for the glass of water on the nightstand. "About last night... Were you really trying to get me kicked out of Spago, or was that just a side bonus?"

"You loved it," she purred, twirling a lock of his hair between her fingers. "The way all those women were watching you, the way they whispered. You were the center of attention, baby. And let's be honest, you thrive on that."

"Yeah, well, I don't usually thrive shirtless on a table with a sparkler in my teeth," he muttered, though the corner of his mouth twitched in amusement.

"Oh, come on," Brittany cooed, tracing her nails lightly down his chest. "You're my little show pony. What's the harm in giving people a show?"

He arched a brow, his voice dropping. "Show pony, huh? That's what this is to you?"

She smirked, unbothered by the edge in his tone. "Let's not pretend you're here out of love and devotion, darling. You like the trips, the champagne, the shopping sprees. And you definitely like the lifestyle. Don't act like it's a one-way street."

"Fair enough," he admitted, though there was a flicker of something darker in his eyes. Resentment, maybe. Or shame.

Brittany shifted closer, her lips brushing his collarbone. "You're not just arm candy, Brad. You're the perfect distraction. And let's face it, I'm the best thing that's ever happened to you."

"Best thing, huh?" he said, his voice laced with sarcasm. "Tell that to my pride."

"Oh, baby," she murmured, pressing her body against his. "Pride doesn't pay the bills."

Their lips met in a clash of heat and ego, a kiss that was as much about power as passion. Bradford pulled back first, his breathing ragged. "You're dangerous, Britt. You know that?"

"And you love it," she shot back, a wicked glint in her eye.

He couldn't argue with that.

The moment was interrupted by the chime of her phone. Brittany reached for it, scanning the screen before a sly smile spread across her face. "Belize is confirmed," she said, scrolling through her emails. "And Dubai's after that. I hope you're ready for the ride."

"Dubai," he repeated, his tone flat. "Another gallery opening? Or just an excuse to show me off?"

"Both," she admitted shamelessly. "And trust me, you'll thank me when we're on the beach with mojitos in hand."

He shook his head, a reluctant smile tugging at his lips. "You're unbelievable."

"I know," she said with a wink, tossing her phone aside. "Now, let's talk about what you're wearing. I'm thinking something tight, tailored, and scandalously expensive. You'll be the envy of every man in the room—and every woman too."

Bradford laughed, though it was tinged with exasperation. "You've got this whole thing planned out, don't you?"

"Of course," she said, straddling his hips. "That's what I do. And you? You're just along for the ride."

For a moment, he looked like he might protest, but then her lips were on his again, silencing the flicker of defiance before it could fully form. It was always like this—any time he started to push back, Brittany would find a way to pull him under, drowning his resistance in silk sheets, expensive cologne, and the heady rush of being desired.

As the morning sun bathed the penthouse in golden light, the Strip below stirred with its own brand of artificial life. Neon signs, once defiant in the night, now flickered weakly in the face of daybreak, their magic fading in the cold, indifferent dawn. It was a city built on illusion, a playground where fantasy masqueraded as reality, and somewhere in that delicate deception, Bradford had lost track of where he fit.

He lay still, watching the light shift across the ceiling, tracing the jagged edges of his own reflection in the mirrored panels above the bed. He'd had younger women before—models with dewy skin, coeds with tight bodies and empty heads, party girls with daddy's credit card and a hunger for beautiful distractions. Brittany wasn't them. She was in her thirties, still striking, still elegant, but no longer untouchable in the way twenty-two-year-old starlets were. Time had softened her, just a little. There were fine lines at the corners of her eyes, a touch of something desperate in the way she clung to youth with Botox and discipline.

But none of that mattered. Because unlike those other women, Brittany worshipped him.

She didn't treat him like a disposable thrill, didn't giggle and flirt while already eyeing someone richer, more powerful. She fed him the finest meals, draped him in tailored suits, whispered in his ear like he was the most exquisite thing she'd ever owned. Being a boy toy treated like a king was better than being just another handsome face, another forgettable conquest in a sea of pretty distractions.

And yet, the thought lingered—how long before she moved on? Before his body, his face, his charm stopped being enough?

Brittany stretched beside him, her body languid and feline, her emerald-green eyes flicking toward him with amusement. "You're thinking too hard," she murmured, tracing a lazy finger down his chest. "That's not your job, sweetheart."

His jaw tightened, but he forced a smirk, the kind that kept the illusion intact. "Right. Wouldn't want to ruin the aesthetic."

She grinned, pressing a kiss to his shoulder. "Exactly. Now, be a doll and pour me a mimosa. We have a long day of being fabulous ahead of us."

Bradford exhaled slowly, reaching for the bottle of Dom perched on the nightstand. As he popped the cork, watching the golden liquid fizz and spill over the rim, he wondered—not for the first time—if this was all he'd ever be.

A well-kept secret. A walking indulgence.

A man playing a role in a game where he wasn't sure he even knew the rules.

But in Vegas, where reinvention was always one gamble away, he told himself that maybe—just maybe—he still had a few cards left to play.

For now, though, he poured the drink, plastered on a smile, and let the performance continue.

CHAPTER 7: POWDERED LIES AND SWEET REVENGE

The Downtown Cocktail Lounge was dimly lit, its moody ambiance creating a haze of soft light that bounced off vintage chandeliers. The scent of whiskey, citrus, and expensive perfume mingled in the air, setting the tone for a Friday night where secrets would inevitably spill as easily as the drinks. Coco Rivera walked in, her heels clicking against the polished concrete floor, her tight black dress hugging every curve. Her hair, sleek and raven-dark, cascaded down her back, and her sharp hazel eyes scanned the room like a predator looking for her next move.

At the bar, Megan Davenport leaned against the counter, sipping a cocktail that matched her meticulously polished aesthetic. Her long blonde hair shimmered under the dim lighting, her short white dress exuding effortless allure. Coco caught sight of her and felt a twinge of annoyance, but she smirked, masking her irritation with a confident stride toward the bar.

"Megan," Coco purred, her voice dripping with faux warmth. "Long time, no see."

Megan glanced up, her green eyes narrowing slightly before her lips curled into a tight smile. "Coco. What a surprise. Didn't expect to see you here."

Coco tilted her head, her expression playful. "Vegas isn't that big, darling. You're bound to run into people."

Megan gestured to the bartender. "Let me get you a drink."

Coco raised an eyebrow but slid onto the stool next to Megan. "How generous. What's the occasion?"

Megan sipped her cocktail, leaning in slightly. "Let's just say I'm in the mood to celebrate... or commiserate. You pick."

The tension between them was palpable, the kind of undercurrent only two women with a history of competition could create. The bartender placed a gin and tonic in front of Coco, and she lifted it to her lips, never breaking eye contact with Megan.

After a few minutes of idle chit-chat, Megan leaned closer, her tone dropping to a conspiratorial whisper. "Wanna go powder our noses?"

Coco smirked, setting her glass down. "Lead the way."

Inside the bathroom, the sound of a leaky faucet echoed off the tile walls. Megan locked the door behind them and pulled a sleek metal snuff bullet from her clutch. "Imported," she said with a wink, holding it up as if it were a trophy.

Coco crossed her arms, watching as Megan tapped a bump onto the back of her manicured hand and inhaled sharply. Megan exhaled with a satisfied sigh before handing the bullet to Coco.

"Your turn," Megan said, her voice tinged with a challenge.

Coco took the bullet, her movements slow and deliberate. She loaded a bump, sniffing it with practiced ease, her expression unreadable.

"So," Megan began, leaning against the sink. "You heard about

Brittany, right?"

Coco glanced at her, her hazel eyes narrowing slightly. "What about her?"

Megan smirked, her lips curling wickedly. "She was hooking up with Kyler before he went to jail. I'm sure you knew, though."

The words hit Coco like a slap, but she didn't flinch. Instead, she let out a low laugh, handing the snuff bullet back to Megan. "Good for her," she said coolly. "Kyler's will fuck anything that walks and is going to be locked up for a long time."

Megan tilted her head, studying Coco. "You're taking this well. I wasn't sure if you'd... you know, care."

Coco's smile was sharp, almost predatory. "Why would I care? Brittany can have my leftovers."

Megan chuckled, shaking her head. "You're something else, Chloe."

Coco pulled out her own snuff bullet, a sleek black one, and offered it to Megan. "Here, try mine. It's better."

Megan didn't hesitate, loading another bump. She sniffed it quickly, her pupils dilating almost instantly. "Damn, you weren't kidding," she said, her voice tinged with awe.

Coco's smirk deepened. "I never do."

As they left the bathroom, Coco lingered behind, watching Megan saunter off toward her usual crowd. Coco's mind raced, but outwardly, she remained composed. She made her way to the coffee station near the bar, where a neat display of sugar packets sat waiting. Her fingers deftly swept the packets into her clutch, her movements smooth and unnoticeable.

The night air was crisp as Coco stepped out into the parking lot. Megan's white Range Rover gleamed under the fluorescent lights, practically begging to be defiled. Coco opened her clutch, pulling out the sugar packets. She unscrewed the gas cap, one manicured finger tapping the packets of granules into the tank with meticulous precision.

"Sweet dreams," she muttered under her breath, screwing the cap back on and walking away without a second glance.

The next morning, Megan stood beside her immobilized car, her hair disheveled, her white dress from the night before wrinkled. She furiously dialed Brayden, pacing back and forth in the parking lot.

"Pick up, pick up, pick up," she muttered, holding the phone to her ear. The call went to voicemail. "Damn it, Brayden. Where are you?"

Unbeknownst to her, Brayden's phone sat on silent in the locker of a men's bathhouse, far from her drama.

Megan threw her phone into her bag with a frustrated sigh, glaring at her unresponsive car. Somewhere across the city, Coco sipped her morning coffee with a smug smile, savoring her small victory.

CHAPTER 8: HEAT BENEATH THE SURFACE

The glow of neon signs from the strip flickered against the wet pavement as Kimber adjusted her oversized sunglasses, stepping out of the sleek black SUV. The soft hum of traffic filled the air, interspersed with the occasional click of her designer heels. She had just finished her red light therapy session at the boutique spa next door when a familiar figure caught her eye.

Brayden.

Kimber paused mid-step, her sharp green eyes narrowing as she watched him disappear into the entrance of a discreet Korean bathhouse. Her lips curled into a sly smirk as her mind raced. "Well, well, what do we have here?"

The bathhouse entrance was understated, almost easy to miss—unassuming signage and frosted glass. Kimber, ever the predator, followed with a confident stride, her body wrapped in a tight-fitting leather jacket over a crop top and jeans that hugged her curves in all the right places.

Inside, the air was humid, carrying the faint scent of eucalyptus and cedarwood. Brayden stood by the front desk, his tailored jacket slung casually over his shoulder, his polished loafers slightly out of place against the minimalist décor of the bathhouse. He was mid-conversation with the attendant when Kimber sidled up beside him, her presence immediately commanding attention.

"Fancy seeing you here, Brayden," Kimber purred, her voice dripping with faux surprise. She leaned casually against the counter, the scent of her floral perfume cutting through the steamy air.

Brayden stiffened, glancing sideways at her. "Kimber," he said flatly, clearly unamused. "What are you doing here?"

"Red light therapy next door," she replied, letting her lips curve into a playful smile. "You know, self-care and all that. But you... I had no idea you were the type to frequent a bathhouse."

Brayden raised an eyebrow, his tone clipped. "It's relaxing. You should try it."

"Oh, I think I will," Kimber teased, her eyes gleaming. She stepped closer, her hand brushing against his arm. "Or maybe I'll just stick around here with you. You look like you could use a little relaxation... maybe even a personal massage?"

Brayden pulled his arm away subtly, his jaw tightening. "I'm fine, Kimber. Thanks."

Kimber tilted her head, feigning innocence. "Come on, Brayden. We're all adults here." Her voice dropped to a whisper as she leaned in, her lips grazing his ear. "No strings, no drama. Just a little... stress relief."

Brayden stepped back, putting deliberate distance between them. "Not interested," he said firmly, his blue eyes locking onto hers. "And even if I were, I don't mix business with whatever this is."

Kimber blinked, momentarily taken aback. Then, her lips twisted into a smirk, masking her surprise. "Well, that's a first. No man has ever turned me down before."

"There's a first time for everything," Brayden shot back, his tone icy.

Kimber studied him, her green eyes narrowing as if piecing together a puzzle. "You know," she began, her voice lilting with mock curiosity, "it's funny. A guy like you turning down... this," she gestured to herself, "makes me wonder."

"Wonder what?" Brayden asked dryly.

"Oh, I don't know," Kimber replied, her smirk widening. "Maybe you're not as into Megan as you pretend to be. Maybe you're not into women at all."

Brayden's expression hardened, his posture straightening. "Watch it, Kimber."

"Relax," she said, waving a manicured hand. "I don't care who you are or aren't into. But Megan? She might care. And your clients? They might care too."

Brayden's lips curled into a humorless smile. "You're really something, Kimber. You think throwing baseless accusations around gives you leverage?"

Kimber shrugged, her demeanor playful but her eyes calculating. "I think knowing secrets makes life more... interesting."

Brayden crossed his arms, his voice dropping to a professional monotone. "Speaking of leverage, let's talk about Kyler. His charges are serious, Kimber. I'm going to need another $12,000 to continue building a defense."

Kimber's eyes widened slightly. "Twelve grand? You've got to be kidding me."

"Not kidding," Brayden replied smoothly. "This isn't a minor offense, Kimber. It's assault and narcotics possession. If you want me to get him out on bail and keep him out, that's the cost."

Kimber hesitated, her playful façade cracking slightly. She tapped her nails against her phone, considering her options. Finally, she sighed and opened her Zelle app. "Fine. You get six now. I'll send the rest next week."

Brayden watched as the transaction went through, his expression unreadable. "Pleasure doing business with you."

Kimber leaned closer, her smirk returning. "You're lucky you're good at what you do, Brayden. Otherwise, I might've been tempted to ruin you."

Brayden's smile was razor-sharp. "And you're lucky I don't bill for every second you waste with these games."

As Kimber turned to leave, she glanced back over her shoulder, her eyes gleaming with mischief. "Oh, and Brayden? If you ever change your mind... you know where to find me."

Brayden exhaled sharply, shaking his head as she disappeared through the frosted glass doors. The air in the bathhouse seemed to grow heavier as he rubbed his temples, bracing himself for the chaos Kimber inevitably left in her wake.

CHAPTER 9: AN OVERT HATER

Sand Dollar Lounge – Bradford and Jase

The Sand Dollar Lounge was a melting pot of dimly lit charm and shadowy pretension. The cracked leather booths and glowing amber bar lights felt timeless, though the musky scent of spilled bourbon and decades-old varnish grounded it in a gritty present. A blues band strummed lazily in the corner, the smoky melody weaving through murmured conversations and the clinking of glasses.

In the back booth, Bradford leaned comfortably, his whiskey sour balanced loosely in his hand. The slight tilt of his head and the smirk tugging at the corner of his mouth gave him an air of unbothered confidence. Draped casually over the booth beside him was a tailored blazer—subtle, expensive, and quietly proclaiming he didn't need to be loud about his status.

Across from him, Jase swirled his bourbon with practiced indifference, his eyes darting around the room, evaluating the worth of everyone he saw. He wore a well-fitted shirt, sleeves rolled up to reveal toned forearms, the kind of casual effort designed to suggest he wasn't trying too hard, even though he always was.

"So," Jase drawled, leaning back as if settling in for a show.

"Belize, huh? Must be nice to play the part of Instagram boyfriend. Designer luggage, first-class flights, the whole 'boy toy for hire' package. Brittany's got you looking like a walking tax write-off."

Bradford's smirk widened, and he raised his glass in a mock toast. "Better to be a tax write-off than someone still handing out comp lists at the door of a club that peaked a decade ago." He sipped his drink slowly, letting the dig sink in.

Jase's smile was tight, his laugh barely audible over the music. "Touché. But let's be honest—you're not fooling anyone. Brittany's not keeping you around for your charm. She's banking on you to make her look like she's still got it. And maybe you're fine being her little PR stunt, but don't act like it's something more."

Bradford chuckled, shaking his head. "You think I care what it looks like? I'm flying out tomorrow, Jase. To Belize. After that, Spain. Then Tulum and Dubai. Meanwhile, you're here trying to impress tourists with a free bottle of Tito's."

Jase leaned forward, his elbows on the table, his voice dropping a notch. "Flying out on her dime, you mean. Let's not get it twisted. You're only standing on that pedestal because she's holding it up for you. Without Brittany, you're just another washed-up DJ looking for a handout."

Bradford's grin didn't falter, but the spark in his eyes sharpened. "And without those door lists and fake smiles, what are you, Jase? Just another guy who peaked in the Vegas hustle and never figured out how to climb past it."

The tension crackled like static electricity. Jase's smirk slipped for just a moment before he leaned back, taking a deliberate sip of his bourbon. "I'll take the hustle over playing kept boyfriend any day. At least I've got my pride."

Bradford barked a short laugh, shaking his head. "Your pride? The same pride that had you shacking up with Tammy and Coco? Let's be real, man—those weren't even low-hanging fruit. Those were rotten fruit that fell off the tree and rolled into the gutter."

Jase's jaw tightened, but he forced a grin, masking his irritation. "Never dated either of them. Tammy was a Tuesday-Wednesday special, and Coco... well, let's just call that a lapse in judgment. Not that you're in a position to judge. Word is you and Tammy had a little late-night reunion at Dino's last month."

Bradford's gaze hardened, the humor draining slightly from his expression. "Nice try. But I don't hook up with women who mistake desperation for charm. That's your specialty."

Jase's voice turned icy, his words cutting. "And yet, here you are, propping up Brittany's ego like some rent-a-date, smiling for the camera while she tries to convince the world she hasn't hit her expiration date."

Bradford set his glass down with deliberate care, standing slowly. His movements were calm, but his eyes burned with quiet disdain. "You can keep talking, Jase. Keep throwing those digs. But let's not forget who's flying out of this town tomorrow and who's still here, circling the drain with the same bottle rats you've been chasing since 2015."

Jase stayed seated, his expression neutral but his knuckles white against the glass in his hand. "Enjoy Belize, man. Just remember— when Brittany finally gets bored of her little charity project, you'll be right back here, spinning for tips and hoping someone still remembers your name."

Bradford paused at the door, turning slightly, his smile sharp and cutting. "And when that happens, I'll still be doing better than you, Jase. See you around."

As the door closed behind Bradford, Jase took another sip of his bourbon, the taste bitter against his tongue. Across the room, the blues band played on, oblivious to the silent war that had just unfolded in their midst.

CHAPTER 10: GAMES IN THE SHADOWS

The Sand Dollar Lounge exuded a sultry ambiance that felt like a secret whispered to the night. The dim, golden glow of vintage sconces danced across the walls, illuminating framed posters of blues legends and instruments suspended like relics of another time. A smoky haze hung in the air, mingling with the faint aroma of spilled whiskey and citrusy cleaner. The steady hum of chatter competed with the occasional clink of glasses, while the soft echoes of a blues guitarist packing away his gear lingered in the corners.

Blansten hunched over the bar, his thick-rimmed glasses sliding down his nose as he stared into the amber depths of his beer. The condensation beaded along the glass, pooling into a small ring on the polished wood. He barely noticed Gerde until she dropped onto the stool beside him, her presence like a storm rolling in.

Her platinum blonde hair was piled into a loose bun that seemed haphazardly constructed, strands spilling out like threads of frustration. Her red lipstick, slightly smeared, hinted at hours of drowned sorrows. She wore a sleek, sleeveless black top and tight jeans, her earrings catching the dim light with each animated movement.

"Blansten," she said with a dramatic sigh, the word dripping with exasperation. She waved the bartender over, her manicured nails tapping rhythmically on the counter. "Why does Jase only call me when he's drunk on Tuesdays and Wednesdays? Like, what is that about?"

Blansten turned his head slowly, his glasses reflecting the muted glow of the bar's neon sign. His expression was one of practiced indifference, though the faint creases around his mouth betrayed his exhaustion. "Maybe because he knows you'll pick up," he said flatly, his voice low but pointed. "You let him do it."

Gerde's scowl deepened as she leaned back against the stool, crossing her legs with a huff. Her drink arrived—a whiskey sour with a perfectly twisted orange peel. She took a long sip, her crimson lips leaving a faint mark on the glass.

"I'm not a damn sidepiece," she muttered, swirling the ice in her drink. "He's such a player, isn't he?"

Blansten raised an eyebrow, his lips curling into a wry smile. "He's a host, Gerde. It's literally his job to make everyone feel special. You think you're the only one he's stringing along?"

Her laughter was sharp and bitter, cutting through the lounge's low murmur. "You think I don't know that? I just... I thought maybe I was different."

Blansten sighed, his fingers tracing the rim of his glass. The cool moisture clung to his skin, grounding him in the surreal conversation. "You deserve better," he said quietly. "Someone who actually gives a damn."

Gerde snorted, her smile turning sardonic. "Oh, like you? Don't act like you're not paying Elizabeth for her 'time.'"

Blansten flinched, his shoulders tensing as a flush crept up his neck. He shifted uncomfortably, his eyes darting to the untouched napkin beneath his drink. "That's... different," he mumbled.

"Sure it is," Gerde said, her voice dripping with mock sweetness.

She took another sip of her drink, her gaze locking on his. "We're all just playing games in this town, Blansten. You, me, Jase, even Elizabeth. The difference is... some of us are better at it than others."

Before Blansten could respond, a low, sultry laugh cut through the air. He turned his head and saw Elizabeth, seated in a corner booth draped in shadows. Her legs were crossed elegantly, the slit of her dark dress revealing just enough to tease. The dim light danced off her long, raven hair, and her lips, painted in a deep, vampy red, curved into a knowing smile.

She raised a single finger, beckoning Blansten with an almost hypnotic allure. Her eyes, sharp and gleaming like polished onyx, bore into him, pulling him toward her as if she were weaving an invisible thread. The faint scent of her perfume—floral with a sultry musk—wafted through the air, sending a shiver down his spine.

Blansten hesitated, his pulse quickening. Gerde smirked beside him, her earlier bitterness replaced by amusement. "Well, there's your better," she quipped, swirling her glass.

He stood slowly, his legs feeling unsteady as he moved toward Elizabeth. The polished leather of his shoes tapped softly against the wood floor, each step amplifying the tension curling in his chest. When he reached her booth, Elizabeth leaned forward, her perfume enveloping him fully. Her fingers brushed lightly against his wrist as she motioned for him to sit.

"You've been quiet tonight," she purred, her voice low and intimate, as if they were sharing a secret the world wasn't allowed to hear.

Blansten swallowed hard, the warmth of her touch lingering on his skin. "Just... a lot on my mind," he stammered, his voice barely audible.

Elizabeth's lips curled into a knowing smile. She leaned closer, her voice a soft whisper. "Well, I'm here to help you forget. For a price, of course."

Blansten's heart thudded heavily as he slid into the booth, the scent of her hair intoxicating and the gleam in her eyes both inviting and dangerous. In that moment, the rest of the world seemed to fade, leaving only the games they played and the shadows they shared.

CHAPTER 11: A TRANSACTIONAL AFFAIR

Blansten's one-bedroom apartment was a stark contrast to the glamorous world Elizabeth moved through effortlessly. The small, dimly lit space smelled faintly of old coffee and the citrusy cleaning wipes he'd used in a hurried attempt to tidy up. A half-empty bottle of whiskey sat on the kitchen counter, the amber liquid glowing under the harsh fluorescent light. The muffled hum of the city outside seeped through the closed windows, punctuated by the occasional blare of a car horn or distant siren.

Blansten sat stiffly on the edge of his unmade bed, his palms damp against his jeans. His heart pounded in his chest, each beat echoing the doubts swirling in his mind. He glanced at the cracked digital clock on the nightstand—it was 11:47 PM. She was late, but that was Elizabeth. She arrived on her own terms, always in control, always holding the upper hand.

The faint click of her heels in the hallway sent a jolt of nervous energy through him. A moment later, she appeared in the doorway, her presence filling the room like a gust of perfumed wind. Elizabeth wore a tight black dress that shimmered subtly under the dim light, clinging to her every curve like a second skin. Her long, toned legs ended in sky-high stilettos, the patent leather gleaming with every step. Her dark hair was swept into loose waves that framed her face, and her lipstick was a deep, sultry red that seemed to command attention.

"Blansten," she said smoothly, her voice low and velvety as she closed the door behind her. She set her clutch on the small table by the entrance, her movements deliberate and calculated.

Blansten swallowed hard, his throat dry. "Elizabeth," he managed, his voice barely above a whisper.

She glanced around the room, her sharp eyes taking in the hastily cleaned surfaces and the fresh flowers he'd awkwardly arranged in a chipped vase. A faint smirk played on her lips, equal parts amusement and dismissal.

"Cute," she said, her tone dripping with irony. "You really spruced the place up for me."

Blansten flushed, his fingers fidgeting with the edge of the blanket. "I just... wanted it to be nice for you."

Elizabeth crossed the room, the click of her heels sharp against the hardwood floor. She stopped in front of the mirror mounted above his dresser, adjusting the strap of her dress and applying a fresh coat of lipstick. The faint scent of her perfume—something expensive and floral with a hint of musk—wafted toward him, intoxicating and overwhelming.

"You got the money?" she asked, her tone casual, as if she were asking for the time.

Blansten nodded quickly, reaching into his pocket and pulling out a crumpled wad of cash. He smoothed the bills nervously before handing them to her. "Nine hundred. Just like we agreed."

Elizabeth took the money without hesitation, her manicured nails brushing lightly against his trembling hand. She counted the bills with the precision of a bank teller, her expression unreadable.

Satisfied, she tucked the money into her clutch and turned back to him with a smile that didn't quite reach her eyes.

"See? That wasn't so hard," she said, her voice honeyed but distant.

Elizabeth slipped off her clothes, standing nude over Blansten. She bent over, pulling down her panties, showing him the goods. She turned around, got on her knees, and began to unbutton his pants. She leaned in, sticking out her tongue for him to suck on. He did. Her hands were deft in getting off his belt, skivvies, pants, and shoes.

His solid prick was standing at attention at the sight of her. She slid her hands up his legs, acquainting herself with the rest of him. She broke from the passionate dance of tongues and started sucking on his nipples while her hands teased and probed his shaft and tight balls. She could feel his heart thumping in his chest. She spit on her hands and began to rub her soft pink pussy.

"I am already dripping for you, Blansten," said Elizabeth, staring at his cock like a flesh-starved, mythological nymph. Then she locked eyes with him while squeezing his veiny pole. "I am going to put it in my mouth now, baby," she said, moving further down him.

She pulled her saliva into her mouth and dripped it all over him, gripping his base and wrapping her thick lips around his well-groomed piece. She then began to lick the hot underside of his smooth cock, playing with the spit pile she had built up. Once he was lubed up in her saliva, she put him all the way down her throat, pulled herself off, and went back down on it again and again.

He stood up to get a better angle to see her going to work on him.

"Blansten, you can push my head down on your cock," she said.

He grabbed her by the hair and pressed as she moved up and down like a piston on his pistol. Then he pulled her up by the hair and bent her over the side of the bed. He open-palm spanked her to see how she'd respond.

"You can hit me harder, baby," she purred.

He pulled back and cracked a handprint on her butt cheek.

"Mmmmm… yes, like that, B. I like when you treat me like a slut," she said, looking back over her shoulder.

He spit on his palm and rubbed it on her warm pink juicy gash.

With his cock dripping in her spit, he slowly lowered it into her.

Her breathing became deeper.

He placed his hands on her hips and began thrusting her sweltering hole and watching her milky freckled skin ripple. He felt getting wetter and pulsing around him.

Their juices dripping down to the floor. As his grip got tighter on her, she would gasp in ecstasy, "Like that B, keep squeezing me and spreading my ass, uh that feels so good." He kept pounding her from the back and eventually she came pressing his cock out her and squirting all over the floor.

He then flipped her on her back at the edge of the bed while he stood there holding her ankles up. "Are you ready for more of this dick, you dirty little cum slut?" said Blansten with bolstered vigor from making her climax like a tsunami hitting the apartment.

He entered her again finding the angle while she played with her right nipple and her clit with the other hand. He clinched ankles as he pumped her with a pent up aggression that turned her on. Her eyes got big as he spit on her hand landing on her fingertips making every motion faster. He pushed her legs back further to hit it deeper and her gasps became quicker and heavier. "I am going to cum again," she said with urgency, "keep fucking me like that B," and so he did. She came again even harder push him out of her and squirting again and began to shake and thus came the rolling orgasms. She sat there for a few minutes, allowing the sex tremors to engulf her entire being. Once she gained some semblance of consciousness she turned around and started deep throating his cock. "I want you to cum in my mouth, baby," she said adamantly. As she worked his pole like a seasoned pro, never breaking eye contact for a second, the saliva build up was messy. Her mascara was running down her cheeks from the tears of extasy she felt humming so hard and about to make him bust. "You want this cum? You want it, you dirty girl. I am going to give to you," said Blansten. "Yeah, baby, give me that big fat load. I wanna taste it. Give me all of it," urged Elizabeth. He stood there over her jerking it now with her tongue out and her hand tickling his balls lightly. "Give it to me. Give me that cum, B," she begged, and he did. He grabbed her by the back of the head, thrusting his cock down her throat, busting his baby-batter on her tonsils. "Ahhhhh," he said with his eyes rolling back and sweat pouring down his body. He pulled out of her mouth and looked at her. She was smiling up at him in a sex crazed sweat, milking his dick to get every last drop. He shook. "It so sensitive after," he said. "I know that's why i like it," she said, wiping her messy hands on his sweaty body then licking her fingers. "You taste so good baby," said Elizabeth, "I love the way you fuck me." She rolled over on the bed and he landed next to her. The hot condensation between them was palpable. "I came so hard," he said. "I know. I could feel it shooting out and you kept going. Speaking of going. I gotta get going, B," she said.

Blansten's gaze lingered on her, his chest tightening with a mix of longing and despair. "Do you..." he hesitated, the words catching in his throat. "Do you ever feel anything? For me?"

Elizabeth froze for a moment, her face a mask of perfect indifference. Then she leaned down, her perfume enveloping him as her lips brushed his cheek—a fleeting, calculated gesture that sent icicles right through him as she picked up her clothes off the ground and began getting dressed.

"You're sweet, Blansten," she murmured, her breath warm against his skin. "But feelings? They cost extra."

Her words hung in the air like smoke, their sharpness cutting through him. Blansten watched as she straightened, her heels clicking against the floor as she walked toward the door. The faint creak of the hinges and the soft thud of the door closing behind her were the only sounds in the room now. For a moment, he just sat there, the emptiness of the apartment pressing in around him. The faint scent of her perfume lingered in the air, a cruel reminder of her presence and her absence. He looked down at his hands, his fingers still trembling, and wondered—not for the first time—why he kept playing a game he could never win.

Outside, the city buzzed on, indifferent to his pain. The lights of Vegas glittered in the distance, promising dreams that were always just out of reach. Blansten lay back on the bed, staring at the cracked ceiling, the weight of his choices pressing down on him. Somewhere out there, Elizabeth was slipping seamlessly into another world, leaving him behind in the shadows.

CHAPTER 12: A SHOCKING REVELATION

The Sand Dollar Lounge pulsed with its usual late-night rhythm —a haze of dim amber light softened the edges of the crowded room, where conversations ebbed and flowed like the tide. The air carried the mingled scents of aged whiskey, citrus peel, and the faint musk of too many bodies in too small a space. A sultry melody from the house pianist wound through the room, punctuated by the occasional pop of champagne corks and bursts of laughter from a distant booth.

Elizabeth sat perched on a cracked leather barstool, her sequined dress shimmering with every slight movement, catching the flicker of the neon "Cocktails" sign that buzzed above the bar. Her ruby-red lips curled slightly downward, and her whiskey glass rested in her perfectly manicured fingers, the ice cubes melting lazily. Her legs crossed, her stiletto heel tapped against the brass footrest of the bar, keeping time with the faint jazz tune.

Across from her, Coco Rivera oozed a casual kind of danger. Her dark hair, wild and unruly, framed her face in loose waves that fell like a dark veil over one shoulder. She leaned back in her chair, her posture a studied nonchalance, one leg draped over the other as she swirled the olive in her martini glass. A sly smile played on her lips, a glint of mischief in her hazel eyes that gleamed under the muted light. Her low-cut black top revealed just enough to distract, but not enough to give everything away—a balance she had perfected.

Coco took a deliberate sip of her drink, her gaze locked on Elizabeth. When she finally spoke, her words dripped with honeyed malice. "You're not gonna believe who I saw."

Elizabeth didn't look up immediately, swirling the amber liquid in her glass before responding, her voice low and cautious. "Who?"

Coco leaned forward slightly, letting the moment hang in the air, savoring the tension. "Westin," she purred, watching for the telltale flicker in Elizabeth's expression. "Yeah, your Westin. Guess what? He's back in town, and he's all cozied up with Tiffany."

The name hit Elizabeth like a slap, her body stiffening. Her grip on the whiskey glass tightened, her knuckles whitening as the ice clinked ominously against the sides. "Tiffany who?" she demanded, her voice slicing through the lounge's warm ambiance.

Coco tilted her head, her smile widening as she relished the slow unraveling of Elizabeth's composure. "Tiffany Daniels," she said, dragging out the syllables as if she were savoring them. "You know, bleach-blonde, trashy mouth, probably smells like menthols and bad decisions. She and Westin looked very cozy at Pitbull Ironworks the other night. You know, the same night Kyler got locked up." She leaned back, lifting her martini glass in mock salute. "She's all over him like a cheap suit."

Elizabeth's stomach churned. A sharp, hot anger burned its way up her throat, settling like fire behind her eyes. "You're lying," she hissed, the words barely audible over the noise around them.

Coco raised her hands in mock innocence, the martini glass

precariously balanced between her fingers. "Scout's honor," she said, her voice sweet as poison. "I thought you'd want to know. I mean, it's not every day your MMA ex strolls back into town, arm-in-arm with the queen of bad life choices."

Elizabeth's breath quickened, and her grip on the glass tightened until it seemed the thick tumbler might shatter. Her mind raced with images she couldn't suppress: Tiffany's gaudy laugh, her cheap perfume clinging to Westin's neck, her perfectly manicured claws digging into his arm. The heat of anger and humiliation coursed through her.

"I need some air," Elizabeth muttered, her voice unsteady as she slid off the barstool. The scrape of its legs against the floor was sharp and jarring, drawing a few curious glances from the nearby patrons.

Coco's smirk deepened as she leaned back in her chair, watching Elizabeth grab her clutch with shaking hands. "Don't do anything I wouldn't do," she called after her, her voice cutting through the ambient noise like a blade. The words hung in the air, dripping with challenge and derision.

Elizabeth paused in the doorway, the night's cold air rushing in and biting against her flushed skin. She didn't look back, but her fists clenched tightly around the beaded strap of her clutch. Outside, the Vegas strip glimmered like a mirage—bright, glittering, and full of promises it would never keep. The anger bubbling in her veins felt like both a curse and a lifeline, propelling her into the darkness with only one thought echoing in her mind.

She would find Westin. And she would make sure he never forgot her.

CHAPTER 13: THE JOY OF VIDEO MESSAGE

Tiffany's phone buzzed on the bathroom counter, the vibration rattling against the porcelain sink. Fresh out of the shower, she reached for it absentmindedly, still toweling off her damp hair. When she saw the sender's name, her stomach twisted.

Tammy.

A strange, electric tension snapped through her nerves. She hadn't spoken to that two-faced bitch in years, and yet, here she was. Uninvited. Unwelcome. Tiffany's pulse quickened as her thumb hovered over the notification, a sick feeling curling in her gut.

She tapped the message open. A video.

The thumbnail alone made her skin crawl—dim, foggy lighting, slick bodies entangled. Her breath caught in her throat, fingers tightening around the phone as if gripping it harder would somehow change what she was about to see.

She pressed play.

The sound hit her first.

Moaning.

Not just moaning—Tammy's breathy, drawn-out gasps, that same grating, high-pitched whimper Tiffany had always hated. The acoustics of the gym's steam room made every sound bounce, amplifying the wet slaps of skin against skin. Then, movement. Westin's body shifting, his hands on Tammy's hips, the gleam of sweat slicking his back. His head thrown back in pleasure.

Her **Westin—fucking Tammy.**

Tiffany's heart **plummeted,** a cold, nauseating drop, like the floor had been ripped out from under her. She felt it in her stomach, in her ribs, in the marrow of her bones. A raw, gut-punching betrayal that left her breathless. Her fingers went numb, but she couldn't stop watching. Couldn't look away. The seconds dragged, stretching into an eternity where time ceased to exist—just that bitch's voice, the slap of flesh, and Westin's unmistakable groan, low and satisfied.

Something inside her **snapped.**

Her vision **blurred with red.** A white-hot heat rose from her chest, burning through her throat, her veins, her skull. Her breathing turned ragged, teeth clenched so hard her jaw ached. The edges of the world closed in, like she was seeing through a tunnel, and at the end of it was **Tammy.** Laughing. Gloating.

Fuck no.

Tiffany's body moved on instinct. She threw her towel to the floor, her hands shaking so violently she almost dropped the phone. Her lungs felt too tight, suffocating under the weight of rage, betrayal, and something deeper—**a hollow ache she refused to name.**

Leggings. Sports bra. Sneakers. She shoved her feet into them, her muscles taut, her movements jerky. Her phone almost slipped from her grip as she stabbed at the screen, but she didn't bother texting. Didn't bother calling.

No, this wasn't a conversation.

This was **war.**

She stormed out the door, her pulse drumming like a war cry in her ears.

Westin was at the gym.

And **he was about to fucking regret it.**

Pitbull Iron Works Gym

The gym doors slammed open with enough force to rattle the glass, drawing a few glances from the weightlifters and cardio junkies inside. Tiffany stalked in, her ponytail swinging with every furious step, her breath coming hot and fast. She spotted Westin near the squat racks, mid-laugh at something one of his gym buddies said. Oblivious.

Not for fucking long.

"HEY, WESTIN!" she bellowed, her voice cutting through the pounding bass of the gym speakers.

Westin's head snapped up, his laughter dying the second he saw her. The whole gym seemed to shift, the collective energy tilting in her direction. Heads turned. Whispers started.

Tiffany marched right up to him, chest heaving, fists clenched so tight her nails bit into her palms.

"What the fuck is wrong with you?!" she seethed, shoving him hard in the chest.

Westin stumbled back a step, his hands shooting up in a half-hearted defense. "Tiff, what the hell—"

"You fucked Tammy? TAMMY?!" she shrieked, her voice sharp as broken glass. "That dirty white trash bitch?! Are you actually out of your fucking mind?!"

Westin's face blanched. "Tiff—"

"Oh no, don't 'Tiff 'me! Don't you fucking dare try to smooth this over." Her voice cracked with rage. "I saw the video, asshole."

His jaw locked. "Look, I was—"

"You were what? Horny? Stupid? Both?!" she spat, her eyes burning. "Do you even know what people used to say about her? Huh?"

Westin exhaled sharply, rubbing his face. "Tiffany—"

"She had fucking herpes, Westin! HERPES! And you just went raw-dogging her in a fucking steam room like some nasty-ass porn scene?"

Westin's whole body went rigid. His expression shifted from defensive to horrified.

"Wait—what?"

"Oh, NOW you care?" Tiffany sneered, crossing her arms. "Yeah, there was a rumor back in the day, and guess what? You better pray it wasn't true. You better go get fucking tested before you ever think about touching me again."

Westin ran a hand through his damp hair, his frustration mounting. "Jesus Christ, Tiffany, you're making a scene."

"Oh, you don't like that?" She threw her arms out, turning in a circle to acknowledge the gym patrons now shamelessly staring. "Too fucking bad! Because I just found out my boyfriend—oh wait, ex-boyfriend? Because that's what you are until you get some fucking results back—was slumming it with Tammy-Scammy the Skank of the Earth."

Westin stepped in closer, dropping his voice, laying it on thick. "Tiff, baby, listen to me. She doesn't mean anything. Nothing. I was drunk, I was stupid. I only want you."

Tiffany's nostrils flared. "Drunk? Stupid? Try broke, too." She leaned in, voice dripping with venom. "Because guess what? I'm done paying for your MMA training."

Westin froze. His whole posture changed, the blood draining from his face. "Tiff, come on—"

"No, you come on." She jabbed a finger into his chest. "I pay the rent. I pay for your training. I finance your fucking life. And you go and fuck Tammy Trashcan? In a goddamn steam room?"

Westin took her wrists gently, his voice going honey-sweet. "Baby, stop. Look at me. You know I love you. You're everything to me. You think I'd ever do anything to lose you?"

Tiffany yanked away. "You did! You fucking did, Westin!"

Westin sighed, shaking his head. "Tiff, I swear to God, I'll fix this. I'll do whatever you want. I'll get tested today. I'll never talk to her again. I'll make it up to you."

Tiffany glared at him, shaking with rage. "Oh, you'll make it up to me? How?"

Westin hesitated—just a beat too long.

Sketchy.

Tiffany's eyes narrowed. "What the fuck are you thinking right now?"

Westin exhaled hard, shifting on his feet. "I'll, uh... get some money together. I'll take you somewhere nice. Anywhere you want."

Tiffany scoffed. "Where the fuck is this money coming from? You're fucking unemployed, Westin."

His jaw twitched. "I'll get some fights together and figure it out."

Tiffany studied him, her anger still sizzling under her skin. Liar. Probably planning some bullshit hustle selling steroids or fighting under the table again. Shady, just like always.

Still…

Her heart hammered. Her stomach churned.

She wanted to storm out, leave him standing in his own mess.

But his voice softened again, coaxing, pulling her back in.

"Baby… I only want you. That's it. You're the best thing that ever happened to me." He reached for her hand, his thumb rubbing slow circles over her wrist. "You think I'd ever really want someone else? You're my ride-or-die, Tiff. No one holds me down like you. No one makes me feel the way you do." His voice dipped lower, smooth as silk. "I fucked up, but I need you." His hands slid around her waist. "I can't lose you, Tiff. I won't."

Tiffany exhaled sharply.

She wasn't buying it—not really. But she wasn't done with him yet, either.

Because she was obsessed with him. And she didn't want another woman to have him. She was a possessive stripper-slash-OnlyFans sex worker who knew he was the best she could do in a world of guys that couldn't measure up.

Her life was a constant rotation of sweaty hands, drunk eyes, and empty compliments. But Westin? He was raw. He was hers. And if some gym-rat skank thought she could take what belonged to Tiffany?

Not fucking happening.

She put a hand on his chest, shoving him back one last time. "We are NOT hooking back up until you get tested. That dirty white trash bitch is a fucking plague."

Her lips curled, disgust dripping from every word. "Tammy's been passed around like a blunt at a frat party. She's had more men inside her than a locker room urinal. And you—" She jabbed him in the chest again. "You fell for it like some dumb, desperate rookie? Jesus, Westin. That's fucking embarrassing."

Westin groaned, running his hands down his face. "Fuuuuck. Ugh." He shook his head, staring at the ceiling like it might offer him divine intervention.

Tiffany turned on her heel, not sparing him another look as she stormed away, still within staring distance.

Westin stood there, the weight of his mistake—his stupidity—bearing down on him like a barbell he couldn't lift.

CHAPTER 14: AND ANOTHER ONE

The glaring fluorescent lights of **Pitbull Ironworks Gym** hummed incessantly, throwing their stark, unforgiving glow over every corner of the gritty, industrial space. The tang of sweat, rubber mats, and metal clung heavily to the air, an unrelenting reminder of the hard work being put into every punch, every lift, every bead of sweat dripping onto the worn concrete floor. The rhythmic clash of weights meeting steel racks reverberated through the room, mingling with the low grunts of exertion and the sharp cracks of gloves striking heavy bags.

Elizabeth stepped inside, her stiletto heels clicking against the concrete in a rhythm as sharp as her anger. The usual chatter and clamor seemed to dull as her presence carved through the space. Heads turned; she didn't belong here, not in her sleek black dress that hugged her curves or her hair styled to perfection. But she didn't care. She had a purpose.

Her eyes locked on him almost instantly—**Westin Wexford.** His muscled frame glistened under the harsh lights, tattoos crawling up his arms like intricate battle scars. He moved with precision, sparring shirtless with a partner, the dull thud of gloves meeting flesh punctuating his gruff commands. Elizabeth's chest tightened. For a split second, she saw the man she once loved—the charm, the intensity, the fire in his eyes. But then, like ice water hitting her skin, her gaze shifted to **Tiffany Daniels.**

Tiffany was leaning against a nearby wall, her skintight leggings and neon sports bra accentuating her lithe figure. She laughed obnoxiously into her phone, occasionally glancing at Westin as if staking her claim. Her bleached hair was tied in a high ponytail that swayed with every exaggerated movement, her acrylic nails tapping rhythmically against the screen.

Elizabeth's blood boiled. Her heels clicked louder as she stormed across the gym, a trail of tension following her like static electricity. The clamor of weights and machines seemed to fade, replaced by the rising beat of her own fury.

"**Westin!**" she shouted, her voice cutting through the room like a whip crack.

Westin's head snapped around, his expression flickering from confusion to annoyance in an instant. He dropped his gloves and stepped away from the sparring partner, his chest heaving. "Liz? What the hell are you doing here?"

Elizabeth's eyes burned with betrayal as she jabbed a manicured finger toward him. "What am I doing here?" she repeated, her voice trembling with the force of her anger. "What are **you** doing here? With **her**?"

Tiffany looked up from her phone, her glossy lips curling into a smirk. She pushed off the wall, her toned body moving with the kind of confidence that could only come from knowing she was getting under Elizabeth's skin. "Oh, look, it's the psycho ex. Didn't think you'd show up, but this is better than pay-per-view."

Elizabeth's eyes narrowed, but she ignored Tiffany, her focus locked on Westin. Her voice dropped, low and raw. "You vanished, Westin. No calls, no texts. You left me—like I meant nothing. And now you're back? With **her**?"

Westin sighed, dragging a hand through his damp hair. His sweat-slicked skin glistened in the harsh light, and for a moment, he looked like he was about to say something kind, something apologetic. But instead, his face hardened. "Liz, it's been years. We're done. Move on."

Elizabeth's heart twisted painfully. "Move on?" Her voice cracked, her composure fracturing. "You told me you loved me! You said we'd start over—build a life together!"

Tiffany chuckled darkly, crossing her arms as she sauntered closer. "Wow. Still clinging to that fantasy, huh? Hate to break it to you, sweetheart, but he's with me now. And honestly? He's never looked better."

Elizabeth's fury erupted like a dam breaking. She lunged at Tiffany, shoving her with both hands. "Shut your mouth!" she snarled.

Tiffany stumbled back, her expression flipping from smug to venomous in a heartbeat. "You crazy bitch!" she shrieked, swinging wildly. But Elizabeth was ready, ducking under the blow and clamping down on Tiffany's arm like a vice grip. With a fluid motion, Elizabeth twisted, pulling Tiffany into a tight guillotine headlock. The gym erupted in chaos as onlookers stopped mid-rep, their attention drawn to the spectacle unfolding before them.

"You don't get to talk to me like that!" Elizabeth screamed, her voice echoing off the gym's steel walls. She yanked Tiffany to the ground, pinning her with surprising strength. Straddling her, Elizabeth delivered a series of hammer fists to Tiffany's face, each strike punctuated by a scream of frustration.

"Get off her!" Westin bellowed, sprinting toward them. He grabbed Elizabeth around the waist, hoisting her off Tiffany despite her flailing limbs. Tiffany scrambled to her feet, her face red and bruised, her ponytail disheveled.

"You're dead, bitch," Tiffany hissed, her voice dripping with venom. She reached into her gym bag, her movements frantic but precise. A moment later, she produced a small black taser, its metallic prongs gleaming under the fluorescent lights.

Elizabeth barely had time to react before Tiffany lunged, pressing the taser into her side. The sharp **crackle** of electricity filled the air, followed by Elizabeth's scream as her body convulsed, collapsing to the ground in a trembling heap. Gasps rippled through the crowd as the taser's sharp crackle died away, leaving only Elizabeth's ragged breathing and Tiffany's satisfied smirk.

"Jesus Christ, Tiffany!" Westin shouted, grabbing her arm and yanking her away from Elizabeth. "Are you insane?"

"She started it!" Tiffany snapped, her voice shrill as she wrenched her arm free.

"Police are on their way!" someone called from across the gym.

Westin's eyes darted toward the entrance. "We're leaving. Now," he growled, dragging Tiffany toward the back exit. Tiffany glanced over her shoulder, her bruised face twisted into a victorious sneer.

Elizabeth lay on the cold concrete floor, her body still trembling from the shock. Her vision blurred, but the humiliation burned clear. Above her, the gym's lights glared harshly, mocking her, and the murmurs of the onlookers stung like a hundred tiny cuts. Somewhere in the distance, the wail of approaching sirens cut through the thick air.

CHAPTER 15: POOLSIDE CONFESSIONS

The Red Rock Resort's pool shimmered under the blazing Las Vegas sun, the water catching the light in dazzling ripples. The cabanas stood like small fortresses of luxury, their crisp white curtains billowing lazily in the desert breeze. The faint scent of chlorine mixed with coconut sunscreen lingered in the air, mingling with the murmur of laughter, the clinking of glasses, and the occasional splash of water.

Inside one of the cabanas, Elizabeth reclined on a cushioned lounger, her sequined bikini glinting under the sunlight. She adjusted her oversized sunglasses, her movements languid but deliberate, as though every gesture was a performance. Beside her, Jess sprawled comfortably, her emerald-green one-piece accentuating her toned figure. Her platinum blonde hair gleamed like a beacon, and her lips were painted a daring crimson that popped against her sun-kissed skin.

"You know," Elizabeth began, swirling her glass of sangria, the ice cubes clinking softly, "for all the bullshit this city throws at us, moments like this make it almost worth it."

Jess smirked, tilting her head to catch more of the sun. "Almost. If only the men were half as refreshing as these cocktails."

Elizabeth let out a low laugh, her voice tinged with sarcasm. "Men in Vegas? Please. They're either fragile egos with flashy wallets or washed-up wannabes trying to relive their glory days."

Jess raised her glass in a mock toast. "Here's to that. No point in dealing with their nonsense when we've got each other."

Their glasses clinked, and for a moment, the weight of the world seemed to lift. But then Elizabeth's smile faded, a flicker of tension crossing her face. She set her drink down, leaning forward. "Jess, can I be real with you for a second?"

Jess lowered her sunglasses, her piercing blue eyes locking onto Elizabeth's. "Always, babe. What's on your mind?"

Elizabeth hesitated, her perfectly manicured nails tapping against the glass table. "It's Tiffany. And Westin. I can't let it slide, Jess. She tasered me in front of everyone. In *my home*. Like I'm some nobody. And Westin? Standing there like he doesn't know me? Like I'm nothing?"

Jess leaned back, crossing her legs as she studied Elizabeth. "You're not nothing. Don't let them make you think you are. But what are you planning to do about it?"

Elizabeth's lips curved into a sly smile, the kind that spoke of vengeance calculated down to the last detail. "I'm done letting people like her think they can walk all over me. I need to make a statement."

Jess raised an eyebrow, her expression cautious but intrigued. "What kind of statement?"

Elizabeth leaned in closer, her voice dropping to a conspiratorial whisper. "The kind that comes with a bang."

For a moment, Jess said nothing, her gaze unwavering. Then, with a slow nod, she reached into her oversized bag. From beneath a stack of magazines and sunscreen, she pulled out a small, black object wrapped in a towel. She placed it on the table between them, unwrapping it to reveal a sleek Glock with the serial number filed off.

Elizabeth's breath caught, her eyes narrowing as she reached out, her fingers brushing against the cool metal. "Jess... you came prepared."

Jess shrugged, a wicked grin playing on her lips. "You think I don't know how this city works? Sometimes you have to send a message, and sometimes that message has to be loud."

Elizabeth picked up the gun, turning it over in her hands. The weight of it felt both foreign and familiar, a potent symbol of power. "How much?" she asked, her voice steady.

"Eight hundred," Jess replied smoothly. "And I've got a box of hollow points in the trunk. Consider it a package deal."

Elizabeth didn't hesitate. She pulled out her phone, her fingers moving quickly over the screen. The faint ding of a payment notification confirmed the transaction. "Done."

Jess leaned back, a look of satisfaction on her face. "You know, Elizabeth, I've always admired your style. You're not afraid to take what you want."

Elizabeth smirked, tucking the gun back into the towel and slipping it into her bag. "And you're not afraid to make sure I can."

They sat in companionable silence for a moment, the sun casting a golden glow over the pool. The laughter and chatter of other guests felt like background noise to their quiet understanding.

"You've always had my back, Jess," Elizabeth said finally, her voice softer.

"And I always will," Jess replied, raising her glass. "To bad bitches who refuse to lose."

Elizabeth clinked her glass against Jess's, a genuine smile breaking through her usual guarded expression. "To us."

As the sun began to dip below the horizon, casting long shadows across the pool deck, the two women lounged in their cabana, their bond fortified by the unspoken understanding that in a city as ruthless as Vegas, all you really needed was someone who had your back.

CHAPTER 16: THE COST OF FREEDOM

A thick clang reverberated down the corridor as the heavy metal door slid open, the final gateway between Kyler and the outside world. He stepped through cautiously, his feet brushing the linoleum with the hesitancy of someone testing unfamiliar ground. Behind him, the sounds of jail faded: the echo of shuffling footsteps, low murmurs of bored guards, and the occasional metallic scrape of keys against bars. It was a soundscape he hoped never to hear again, though the imprint of it lingered, etched into his nerves.

The reception area's harsh fluorescent lighting did nothing to soften the edges of his exhaustion. The overhead lights cast sharp, angular shadows across his face, making the hollow beneath his eyes seem cavernous. He hadn't slept properly in days, and every line etched into his features told the story of sleepless nights and gnawing anxiety. His clothes didn't help: a wrinkled, sweat-stained T-shirt and designer sneakers that had seen better days. The once-crisp kicks now looked almost pitiful, the soles scuffed and battered, as though they'd carried the weight of more than just his steps.

Waiting near the exit was Brayden, his lawyer. Dressed in a tailored navy blazer and spotless oxford shoes, Brayden looked distinctly out of place in the dingy confines of county lockup. His meticulously styled hair and the faint scent of cologne trailing him might as well have been a neon sign declaring his detachment from this world. He was the kind of man who thrived in polished corporate offices, not places that reeked of bleach and despair.

Brayden's sharp eyes scanned Kyler as he approached, flicking briefly to his sneakers, then to his jawline—now shadowed with stubble. His expression carried a mixture of relief and caution, like a man relieved his gamble had paid off but wary of the stakes still on the table.

Kyler attempted a smirk, but it barely qualified. "Took you long enough, man." His voice was scratchy, rough around the edges, just like everything else about him at that moment.

Brayden exhaled, his lips pressing into a thin line of feigned patience. "You're welcome, Kyler. Frame that gratitude for me, will you?" His tone was tinged with dry humor, though the weariness in his eyes betrayed how much effort it had taken to get Kyler out of this mess. "The toxicology report came in just in time. Coco's drug screen was a disaster—MDMA, cocaine, and ketamine all in her system that night. The lab tech said it was a miracle she was upright. That, plus her priors, gave us the leverage we needed."

Kyler snorted, running a hand through his disheveled hair. "Classic Coco. The walking pharmacy strikes again." His voice was laced with bitterness, but there was an edge of something deeper —something wounded.

Brayden stepped closer, lowering his voice as if the walls had ears. "It's worse than that, Kyler. She didn't just dabble; she was on a bender. And don't get me started on the 911 call. She put the operator on hold mid-call to chat with one of her friends, then casually clicked back over to report the alleged assault."

Kyler let out a bark of disbelieving laughter. "You're kidding. Please tell me you're kidding."

Brayden shook his head, his expression grim. "I wish I were. The DA's office is still taking her testimony seriously, though. And don't forget—she's got a history of lying to police and theft. Remember her priors? Both tied to casinos, both involving her targeting guests."

Kyler's grin twisted into something darker. "So, what you're saying is, she's a real model citizen?"

Brayden allowed himself a faint chuckle but sobered quickly. "Look, I'm not saying this is a slam dunk. Her testimony's shaky, but you're not out of the woods yet. Bail isn't freedom, Kyler—it's a chance. A chance to prove she's not credible before this goes to trial. Don't screw it up."

The words hung in the air, heavier than the metal doors that had just slammed shut behind them. Kyler nodded, his cocky veneer slipping just enough to reveal a crack of vulnerability. "I hear you. No sneezing near trouble, no parties, no social media stunts. I'll even look both ways before jaywalking."

Brayden rolled his eyes, the corners of his mouth twitching into a reluctant smirk. "A real comedian, aren't you? Save it for court. Maybe it'll charm the jury. For now, let's just get out of here before someone decides to snap a picture of you outside the county jail."

The two stepped out into the cool desert night, the air crisp and clean compared to the stale atmosphere inside. Vegas stretched out before them in neon-lit glory, its electric pulse both seductive and foreboding. This was a city that thrived on second chances, but it also had a way of swallowing people whole.

"My car's down the block," Brayden said, gesturing toward the shadows. "Let's avoid a photo op, shall we?"

Kyler's laugh was dry, his voice carrying a note of self-deprecation. "What am I now, the poster boy for bad decisions?"

Brayden didn't answer immediately, his eyes scanning their

surroundings. "More like the cautionary tale for people who think their money makes them untouchable."

They walked in silence for a moment, the faint hum of distant traffic filling the void. Kyler glanced at Brayden. "Coco...she won't drop the charges, will she?"

Brayden's jaw tightened. "Not a chance. She's holding on to this like her life depends on it. And with her, it probably does. She's fueled by drama, attention, and whatever chaos she can create. But if we play our cards right, the DA will see her for what she is: unreliable, reckless, and dangerous."

Kyler didn't respond. His gaze fell to the pavement, his mind a whirl of frustration and exhaustion.

As they reached Brayden's sleek black sedan, Kyler paused, staring at his distorted reflection in the car's window. Freedom still felt like a fragile thing, as if it could shatter with a single wrong move.

Brayden unlocked the car, and they climbed in. The rich scent of leather replaced the institutional odors that clung to Kyler. Brayden started the engine and glanced at Kyler. "This isn't over. If you want to stay free, we've got a long road ahead. Don't let your pride trip you up."

Kyler leaned back against the seat, the city lights streaking past the window like ghosts of choices made and unmade. For now, he was free—but the cost of freedom was just beginning to tally.

CHAPTER 17: MEETING LORRAINE "LORI THE LESBIAN" DEFALCO

Brayden dropped Kyler off at an abandoned lot near the industrial edge of town, the squeal of the sedan's tires echoing against the deserted warehouse walls. The air smelled like burnt rubber and oil, thick with the sour stench of rotting garbage from a nearby dumpster. The glow from the taillights disappeared into the night, leaving Kyler alone in the shadows.

The night felt alive with an undercurrent of menace. Above him, thick clouds dulled the moonlight, casting the lot in an eerie half-darkness. The distant hum of highway traffic mixed with the occasional drip of water leaking from a busted pipe nearby. A single floodlight buzzed overhead, its sickly yellow glow barely illuminating the cracked pavement below. A gust of wind rattled a chain-link fence, sending discarded fast-food wrappers and cigarette butts tumbling like tumbleweeds.

Kyler stepped forward, slipping behind the looming metal building whose corrugated sides groaned under the wind's assault. His pulse quickened. He was no stranger to places like this—forgotten pockets of the city where deals were made, where debts were settled, where the unlucky went missing.

Against the graffitied wall, beneath the flickering glow of the floodlight, stood Lorraine Defalco—better known as Lori the Lesbian. At first glance, she looked built like a linebacker, the kind of person who could flatten someone with a single hit. The broad shoulders, the thick forearms, the stance that suggested she could take a punch and keep coming. But Kyler knew better. It was an illusion—a trick of oversized hoodies, wide hips, and the sheer mass of her obesity. Underneath the fabric, Lori was less brute force and more sluggish bulk, a woman whose body had long since stopped cooperating with the image she projected. Her movements had the heaviness of someone who still thought they were an athlete but was now weighed down by the reality of their own excess. A patterned bandana held back her slicked hair, and in the dim light, her eyes gleamed like wet tar.

She wasn't just a dealer. She was a fixture in the city's underbelly, a legend in the back alleys where junkies whispered her name like a cautionary tale. Some said she had killed a man for shorting her one hundred bucks. Others swore she ran an operation so airtight that even the cops wouldn't cross her. Kyler knew one thing for certain—Lori didn't tolerate bullshit.

She was scrolling through her phone when he approached, her thumb lazily dragging across the screen. The glow illuminated her face, exposing the softness beneath the tough exterior— puffy cheeks, a double chin she tried to hide with a well-angled bandana. Without looking up, she spoke, her voice a gravelly rasp from years of chain-smoking cheap menthols.

"You got good lawyers, huh?" she muttered, slipping the phone into her pocket. "Didn't expect to see you walking free so soon."

Kyler swallowed the dryness in his throat. "Brayden sorted it."

Lori let out a short laugh, a sound that held no real amusement. Up close, she smelled like stale smoke, cheap cologne, and the unmistakable chemical bite of hard drugs. Her gut strained against the fabric of her hoodie when she shifted, as if she was still trying to stand in a way that made her look powerful rather than just... big.

"Yeah?" She tilted her head, sizing him up. "Word is, you're in deep with that Coco chick. Heard you're out on bail on some... assault charge?"

Kyler's jaw tightened at the mention of Coco. "She's lying. She was high as a kite that night—on coke and amphetamines."

Lori's expression didn't change. Her eyes, dark and unreadable, stayed locked on his. Then, slowly, she pulled a plastic baggie from the pocket of her hoodie. The fine white powder inside caught the light, shimmering like crushed glass.

"This," she said, shaking it slightly, "has a kick to it. So I hear."

Kyler didn't blink. "That the good stuff?"

Lori smirked, her lips pressing into a line of cracked, peeling skin. "Fentanyl's no joke, kid. That's what keeps some of these junkies coming back for more. One heavy pinch, people go night-night."

A cold prickle ran down Kyler's spine. He'd seen it before—the blue lips, the convulsions, the way a body went still like someone had flipped a switch.

"That's what I need," he said, voice steady.

Lori studied him for a beat. The distant wail of a siren howled through the night, stretching out between them like a warning neither would acknowledge. She shifted her weight, her breath heavy from the simple act of standing too long.

"Where's the money, homie?" she asked. "I ain't a charity."

Kyler slipped a wad of bills from his jacket. Crisp hundreds, fresh from the bank, an odd contrast to the grime-streaked world around them. He handed the stack over, watching as Lori flipped through it with practiced fingers. Each rustle of paper seemed to amplify the silence.

Satisfied, she shoved the cash into her hoodie. "Alright, take it. Just remember—if this shit ends up in the wrong place, at the wrong time? That's on you."

Kyler took the baggie, sliding it into his pocket with a calculated calm. It felt thin, fragile, but inside was enough death to change the course of multiple lives. He patted it once, securing it.

"Relax," he said coolly. "I've got it under control."

Lori snorted, though it came out more like a wheeze. "That's what they all say." She turned to leave, but the motion was slow, cumbersome, her bulk shifting uncomfortably under the weight of her own presence. Over her shoulder, she muttered, "Just watch yourself, Ky. Word spreads fast if someone starts dropping dead from your product."

Her heavy footfalls echoed as she disappeared around the corner, swallowed by the darkness. The lot felt even emptier now. The wind howled through broken windows and abandoned loading docks, a spectral whisper that rattled through Kyler's bones.

He exhaled sharply, running a hand through his hair. The weight in his pocket felt heavier than it should. The power inside that baggie could either solve his problems or create a nightmare he'd never escape.

Still, in his twisted logic, it was the best chance he had to ensure Coco wouldn't live to testify against him.

With one last glance at the empty lot, Kyler started moving, the baggie rustling in his pocket with every step—an ever-present reminder that in this city, survival had a price. And tonight, he had paid it in full.

CHAPTER 18: BREAKING INTO THE CASITA

The desert sprawled out like a dead thing under the moon's pale glow, nothing but cracked earth, half-buried shards of glass, and thorny brush stretching in every direction. It was past two in the morning, and Kyler rode down a winding back road outside the city, the glow of Vegas barely a smear of orange on the horizon. Out here, away from the casinos and traffic, the silence pressed against him, thick and absolute.

He killed the engine a good distance from his destination—a rundown casita, slumped at the end of a dirt path like an old drunk nodding off. The porch light flickered erratically, casting sickly yellow shadows over peeling paint and a set of warped wooden steps. A battered screen door hung slightly ajar, as if it had given up resisting the wind.

Kyler muttered under his breath, "Mo's probably out hustling at the gym."

He stepped off, toe tapping the kickstand with a measured softness. The desert air was colder than it should have been, sharp against his skin. Every sound seemed magnified—the crunch of his boots on gravel, the dry whisper of wind through brittle sagebrush. In the distance, the low hum of highway traffic was a dull, distant thing, like blood rushing in his ears.

The porch steps groaned under his weight as he reached the front door. Up close, the place smelled like rot and stale tobacco, something rank seeping from beneath the threshold—old food, mildew, maybe something worse. Kyler pressed a hand to the doorknob. Locked. No surprise.

Reaching into his hoodie pocket, he pulled out a lock pick and wedged it in the slot. A few careful pushes. A crisp snap of the latch. The door sighed open, slow and reluctant.

Inside, the air was thick with the stench of cigarette smoke, sweat, and spilled booze. A single overhead bulb flickered dimly, casting greasy light over the squalor. The couch was covered in cigarette burns and questionable stains. A cheap particleboard table overflowed with empty beer cans, half-eaten takeout, and a crusted-over ashtray. The walls, once white, were yellowed with nicotine, the ceiling fan barely turning, just pushing the stale air around like it was too tired to do its job.

Kyler exhaled through his nose, letting his eyes adjust to the gloom. Slim Mo's place looked exactly how he imagined—filthy, cluttered, stinking of bad choices. He scanned the room, his pulse steady but alert.

"Where would he keep his stash?"

He moved through the living room, stepping carefully over a pile of crumpled fast-food wrappers. A narrow hallway stretched into darkness. The linoleum floor was cracked, curling at the edges, sticky underfoot. To the right, a slightly ajar door revealed a cramped bedroom, just as grimy as the rest of the place. A tiny dresser stood against the wall, its top drawer locked with a cheap padlock.

Kyler clicked his tongue. "Come on..."

He pulled out the lockpick kit from his pocket and went to work. The room was quiet, save for the distant hum of the broken fan. His hands were steady, his breath slow. A few precise movements, a soft metallic click, and the lock popped open.

Inside, a large plastic baggie set inside. The white powder, looking like a bag of baking soda, with little plastic sandwich bags & rubber bands set next to it. A knot tightened in Kyler's gut. Mo had built a solid operational stash. The kind of thing that kept people dead-eyed and dependent.

He reached into his hoodie, pulling out the baggie of fentanyl-laced cocaine Lori had given him. Careful. Measured. He grabbed Slim Mo's bag and opened it, working quickly but methodically. Pouring a hefty sprinkle in, blending the lethal dust with the rest. The powder swirled faintly under the dim glow of a dusty bedside lamp. He held his breath, hyperaware of the danger in every grain.

Sweat prickled at his brow as he zipped the baggie shut, placing it back exactly as it was. His fingers trembled slightly as he latched the drawer again. The weight of what he'd done settled in his chest. Coco Rivera's days were numbered if she got her hands on this. And if she was out of the picture, she wouldn't be testifying.

He stood, flexing his fingers. The room felt smaller now, pressing in. The walls watched him with their nicotine-stained eyes.

Kyler turned back toward the living room. The couch, the table, the overflowing trash—it all felt heavier now. A place steeped in the ghosts of bad deals and desperate people.

A sticky wine glass sat abandoned on the edge of the table, next to a plate still smeared with dried pasta sauce. The smell turned his stomach. Slim Mo had eaten recently. Which meant he might be back soon.

Kyler moved faster, stepping carefully toward the front door. He paused. Listened. Nothing but the steady hum of that busted porch light and the slow creak of the fan. No sound of a car pulling up. No footsteps. Just the empty desert breathing beyond the walls.

He slipped outside, the cold air hitting him like a slap. His chest rose and fell in quick, controlled breaths as he made his way back to the motorcycle. The casita loomed behind him, hunched in the darkness, oblivious to the poison he'd just left inside.

Kyler slid behind the handlebars, his hands tight on the throttle. The ignition turned, headlight cutting through the empty road. The baggie in his hoodie was gone. His work was done.

As he rode toward the distant lights of the city, his heartbeat thundered in his ears. He wasn't sure what felt stronger—the rush of getting away with it, or the gnawing realization that, one way or another, this move had cost him a piece of himself.

Vegas had a way of chewing people up, spitting out what was left. And tonight, he'd bought himself another breath of borrowed time—with someone else's blood on the tab.

CHAPTER 19: A CHANCE OUTCOME

The roar of the Harley Fatboy split the silence of the desert night as Kyler tore down the empty highway, the wind slashing across his face like a blade. His knuckles were tight around the handlebars, veins standing out in stark contrast against the tattoos that inked a quarter of his body. The engine throbbed beneath him, a mechanical heartbeat in sync with his own adrenaline-fueled pulse.

The night stretched wide and endless, a vast expanse of nothingness broken only by the intermittent glow of mile markers and the occasional desolate gas station long past closing. The desert air carried the sharp scent of sage and asphalt, mingling with the lingering musk of sweat and the stale cigarette smoke clinging to his jacket. Every breath he took was dry, sharp, a reminder that he was very much alive—something Slim Mo wouldn't be able to say for long.

He had done it. The bastard's stash was laced, a silent death sentence hidden beneath the promise of a high. It was the kind of justice Kyler knew best—swift, ruthless, and undeniable. And the best part? It wouldn't trace back to him. By the time Coco Rivera got her hands on that blow, she'd be in the ground or the ER, and either way, she wouldn't be showing up in court to put him away.

His jaw clenched as he thought about the way she'd smirked when she made her threats, acting like she had him cornered. No one cornered Kyler. Not a judge, not a dealer, and certainly not some vindictive, power-hungry woman looking to settle a score. He'd spent years building his rep, carving his place in the underground. He wasn't about to let it all come crashing down because of one loose end.

The headlights sliced through the darkness, illuminating the two-lane road that stretched ahead like a black ribbon. His gaze flicked to the rearview mirrors, scanning for any signs of pursuit. No cops, no tail. Just him and the night.

But the feeling of being watched clung to him, a phantom presence pressing against his back. He'd spent too many years looking over his shoulder to believe in clean getaways. He wasn't naive enough to think that karma wouldn't try to collect its dues eventually.

His phone vibrated against his thigh, the buzz rattling in his bones. He ignored it at first, his focus locked on the road, but when it pulsed again, something uneasy twisted in his gut. He risked a glance down, catching Brayden's name glowing against the screen.

Shit.

Brayden wasn't the type to call twice unless it was serious. Kyler hesitated, then let the call go to voicemail. Whatever it was, he'd deal with it when he was damn well ready.

A neon sign flickered in the distance, a run-down 24-hour diner sitting like a relic from a bygone era. The idea of stopping, of slipping into a booth and pretending for a few minutes that he wasn't a man with blood on his hands, was tempting. But the truth was, he couldn't slow down. Not yet. Not until he knew for certain that the pieces were falling into place.

The weight of the decision sat heavy on his shoulders, pressing against his ribs like a vice. He had done a lot of things in his life—things most people wouldn't understand, things he didn't care to explain. But this? This was different. This wasn't just business; it was survival.

A part of him wondered if Coco would even see it coming. If she'd sit there, blissfully unaware, as she took that first lethal hit. Would she realize, in those final moments, that she'd made a mistake? That she'd underestimated him?

He exhaled slowly, forcing himself to shake the thought. It didn't matter. The game was set, and all he had to do now was let it play out.

The Vegas skyline was a distant glow on the horizon, a city built on sins he knew all too well. It called to him like a siren, promising refuge and ruin in equal measure.

Kyler tightened his grip on the throttle, his decision made. He wasn't looking back.

He never did.

CHAPTER 20: COKE AND MIRRORS

The Strip's neon haze bled into the night sky as Coco Rivera weaved through traffic in her battered white sedan, one hand gripping the wheel, the other fumbling with a half-smoked cigarette. The radio sputtered between static and the faint pulse of a hip-hop beat, but she barely heard it. Her mind was tangled in a loop of urgency and withdrawal, a restless energy clawing at her nerves.

Her fingers tapped an impatient rhythm against the steering wheel. Every red light, every slow-moving tourist rental felt like a personal attack. She needed to get to Slim Mo's. Needed to get her hands on something—anything—that could push the creeping sickness away. Her skin itched, and a dull ache curled around the base of her skull. She was coming down, and she didn't have time for it.

The streets turned darker as she left the Strip behind, the city's gaudy lights giving way to the forgotten edges of town. Down a cracked asphalt road, past graffiti-stained walls and flickering streetlamps, she finally reached Slim Mo's place. His casita sat like a forgotten relic at the end of a dirt lane, surrounded by a sagging chain-link fence and the stench of overfilled dumpsters. The only sign of life was the faint thump of bass from inside, rattling the loose window panes.

Coco pulled up, killing the engine but leaving the headlights on, casting long, eerie shadows across the gravel. She took a deep breath, running her fingers through her tangled hair before stepping out. Her boots crunched against the dirt as she approached the front door. The porch light above sputtered weakly, barely illuminating the peeling paint and warped wood.

She knocked, sharp and quick. A moment later, the door cracked open, the chain still latched. Slim Mo's bloodshot eyes peered through the gap, suspicion carved into his face.

"Coco," he grunted, his voice rough from years of chain-smoking. "What do you want?"

She leaned in slightly, letting the chain pull taut between them, a subtle invitation in the way her lips parted. Her voice softened, just enough to make it seem like she wasn't desperate, even though they both knew she was.

"Come on, Mo," she cooed. "You know what I want."

He let out a dry chuckle, shaking his head. "Don't try that with me. I ain't Kyler, and I don't take payment in... pussy."

The dismissal stung more than she let show. Her body language shifted, sultry edges falling away to something more businesslike. If charm wouldn't work, money would.

"Fine," she sighed, fishing into her jacket and pulling out a crumpled wad of bills. "Six hundred, like always."

Slim Mo studied her for a moment before unlatching the chain. The door swung open just enough for her to catch the stale stench of beer, sweat, and something sour lurking beneath. The living room was the same disaster it always was—fast-food wrappers, cigarette butts overflowing in a plastic cup, and a television screen flickering in the background. The place smelled like regret.

"Let's see it," he said, extending his palm.

Coco hesitated for half a second before pressing the cash into his waiting hand. He thumbed through it with practiced ease, nodding to himself before moving to the small end table by the couch. From a drawer, he pulled a plastic baggie, the white powder inside catching the dim light. The sight of it sent a jolt through Coco's veins, a promise that the sick feeling clawing at her insides would soon disappear.

As he handed it over, Slim Mo gave her a long, pointed look. "Don't cause trouble with this," he warned. "Heard rumors. Kyler's out on bail. Cops sniffin 'around. You and him both—y'all need to lay low."

Coco forced a smirk, masking the flicker of anxiety his words sent through her. "Don't worry about me, Mo."

But she should have. Because in her hands, wrapped in that deceptively innocent plastic, was Kyler's insurance policy. Fentanyl-laced coke, a silent death sentence, and she had no idea.

She clutched the bag tight and turned, hurrying back to her car. As she slid into the driver's seat, she let out a shaky breath, her fingers trembling. Relief flooded her chest. She had what she needed. The weight of the world felt a little lighter.

But the devil was already in her hands. And she didn't even know it.

CHAPTER 21: LACED AT THE SAND DOLLAR

The Sand Dollar Lounge pulsed with blues music and hushed conversations. Low lights tinted everything in warm red and amber. Sticky floors, clinking glasses, a swirl of cigarette smoke near the entrance—an ambiance that beckoned both hipsters and washed-up gamblers alike.

Megan Davenport sat at the bar with a small group of friends, sipping a lemon cocktail and tapping her foot to the live band's lazy riffs. She wore a sleek, off-the-shoulder black top, her platinum hair catching the lounge lights. Her phone buzzed relentlessly with notifications—an influencer's life never stopped —but she tried to ignore it for a bit of real-world fun.

In a corner booth, Coco slouched, wearing heavy eye makeup and a disheveled club dress. Her pupils were already pinpricks, and she gripped her little "bullet," a small, refillable metal container for sniffing coke, like it was a holy relic. The hum of the lounge mixed with the throbbing pulse in her ears. The neon sign above the bar flickered in harsh, intermittent flashes, illuminating the sweat beading on her upper lip.

Her heart was already beating too fast—she'd done a few bumps in her car to chase the low. But the cravings demanded more. Without a second thought, she twisted open the bullet, tapped it to her nostril, and inhaled deeply.

She never knew it was laced with a hot dose.

The Overdose

It happened so quickly it almost looked choreographed: One moment, Coco was laughing with half-lidded eyes at nothing in particular, the next, her body stiffened, mouth going slack. A strangled croak escaped her throat, and she collapsed sideways in the booth. The disco lights overhead spun in lazy circles, illuminating her face in ghastly shades of purple and red.

Megan, who was only a few tables away, saw someone leap to their feet and shout. A server dropped a tray of drinks, glass shattering on the floor. Gasps rippled through the lounge as patrons realized something was very wrong.

"She's not breathing! Somebody—help!" a man's panicked voice cut through the noise.

Megan's stomach lurched at the sight: Coco's eyes were half-open, unmoving, a glistening line of foam gathering at the corners of her mouth. Her skin was turning a sickly, ashen blue.

Jase, the V.I.P. club-host after hours scenester hanger-on who thrived on drama, whipped out his phone the instant he heard the commotion.

"Whoa, I gotta get this," he muttered under his breath, hitting "Record." The screen cast a cold glow on his face as he captured every heart-wrenching moment. Coco lay sprawled across the vinyl seat, head lolling, chest frighteningly still.

Megan, adrenaline spiking, dashed over, her heart pounding. She knelt beside the booth as a ring of onlookers formed. Her nose twitched at the stench of booze, spilled cocktails, and pungent sweat. Up close, Coco's lips were turning blue. Megan pressed two fingers to Coco's neck.

"I-I can't feel a pulse!" Megan's voice shook.

Time seemed to slow. Megan's influencer brain took a backseat—instinct from a CPR course kicked in. She dug into her purse with trembling hands, rummaging past lip gloss and phone chargers. She found the Narcan—a dose she'd started carrying after losing a friend to opioids last year.

"Call 911! Now!" she barked.

Someone in the crowd fumbled for their phone, shouting into the receiver. Megan ripped open the Narcan nasal spray. Coco's ragged breathing sounded more like death rattles, froth bubbles at the edge of her mouth. Megan angled Coco's head, steadying her hand.

"Stay with me... come on..." she whispered fiercely.

She administered the Narcan, each second feeling like an eternity. Jase, still rolling his phone camera, edged closer, his expression a twisted mix of fascination and concern.

"Holy... oh man, this is insane," he murmured.

Megan ignored him. Panic coursed through her veins. She checked Coco's pulse again—still nothing. With shaking hands, Megan began chest compressions, pressing down on Coco's sternum in a steady rhythm. The booth's vinyl seat made a squeaking protest with each pump.

"Come on, girl! Breathe!" Megan's voice cracked with desperation.

At last, Coco gave a ragged inhale, jerking slightly as the opioid reversal started to work. Her eyelids fluttered but still refused to open fully. Megan pressed her ear close to Coco's face—there was a shallow, labored breath. Relief mingled with fear in Megan's chest.

"She's breathing," she gasped, barely believing it herself.

Jase turned his phone to himself for a quick reaction shot. "Yo, this girl just almost died right in front of us. Wild night at the Sand Dollar."

Megan shot him a glare so sharp it could cut glass. "Turn that shit off. Right. Now."

For once, Jase hesitated, then lowered his phone. The sound of sirens sliced through the thick Vegas night air. Red and blue lights strobed against the lounge windows as the paramedics arrived. Two EMTs rushed in, pushing past stunned onlookers. Megan moved aside as they set to work, checking Coco's vitals and preparing the stretcher.

As they lifted Coco onto it, one of the EMTs glanced at Megan. "You saved her life tonight," he said.

Megan exhaled sharply, running a shaky hand through her platinum hair. She didn't feel like a hero. She just felt sick.

As Coco was wheeled out into the night, Megan turned back to the lounge, its music still playing, its drinks still flowing, as if nothing had happened. The city never stopped. But Megan knew that somewhere, in the darkness beyond the neon glow, something had just shifted irrevocably.

She pulled out her phone, staring at the endless stream of notifications.

For the first time in a long time, she didn't feel like posting anything at all.

CHAPTER 22: ARRIVAL OF THE AUTHORITIES

The blare of sirens cut through the humid Vegas night, their urgency growing louder as they neared the Sand Dollar Lounge. Through the bar's smudged windows, red and blue lights pulsed in frantic rhythms, painting the walls in alternating streaks of emergency. The scent of spilled liquor, cigarette smoke, and something acrid—fear, maybe—clung to the air as the front door burst open.

A trio of EMTs stormed inside, their uniforms crisp against the lounge's seedy glow. The lead medic, a woman with sharp eyes and an air of practiced control, immediately zeroed in on Coco's barely breathing form slumped in the booth. The crowd, already thick with murmurs, pulled back instinctively, creating a clearing around the scene.

"We'll take it from here—ma'am, thank you," the EMT told Megan, her tone professional but firm.

Megan stumbled back, her limbs trembling from adrenaline. She barely registered the EMTs at work—one tilting Coco's head back to secure the oxygen mask, another checking her vitals, their hands moving with precision. All Megan could see was the way Coco's body looked so small, so fragile, her pale skin marred by the neon light flickering from the bar sign overhead.

A fresh wave of nausea surged in Megan's gut. She had saved her—at least, she hoped she had—but the reality of the moment came crashing down in full force. This wasn't some aesthetic moment to be packaged into a well-lit Instagram post. This was real. Life and death. And she had been the only thing standing between the two.

Then came the news crew.

The Sand Dollar's doors swung open once more, this time admitting a reporter and her camera operator, both tipped off by the police scanner. They wove through the gawkers, eyes sharp, already scenting the story like blood in the water. Their camera's red recording light blinked ominously, locking onto Megan's tear-streaked face.

The reporter thrust a microphone toward her, voice honeyed but firm. "You saved her life tonight. Can you tell us what happened?"

Megan blinked, caught between the past twenty minutes of chaos and the surreal, almost dreamlike quality of a TV interview. Her voice was hoarse when she spoke.

"She... she overdosed," Megan managed, her breath still uneven. "I had Narcan. I just—I couldn't let her die."

She barely noticed the camera zooming in, catching every flicker of emotion in her expression—the glazed-over shock, the relief, the silent terror still lodged in her chest.

From the sidelines, Jase watched it all with growing resentment. His phone was still rolling, but suddenly, it wasn't his moment anymore. He had the footage. He had the best angles, the rawest shots. He had been there first.

And yet, Megan was the one the cameras focused on. Megan was the one getting the recognition.

Jase clenched his jaw, forcing down the bitter taste in his throat.

"This is my video," he muttered under his breath. "I should be the one getting credit."

Viral Sensation

By the time the sun rose over Las Vegas, the video—Jase's video—was already everywhere.

It spread like wildfire across social media, jumping from one platform to the next, accumulating millions of views in mere hours. The thumbnail alone was gripping: the grainy, dimly lit footage of Coco's limp body in the booth, Megan's frantic movements as she administered Narcan, the moment Coco's chest heaved with life again. The perfect storm of tragedy, heroism, and raw, unfiltered drama.

Jase had expected the rush. He had expected the shares, the comments, the virality.

What he hadn't expected was Megan to become the face of it all.

News articles popped up almost instantly, hailing Megan as the "Influencer Good Samaritan" who had saved a woman from an opioid overdose. Hashtags flooded timelines: #NarcanSaves #HeroAtTheBar #GoodSamaritanInfluencer. Her follower count nearly doubled overnight, each refresh showing an influx of likes, comments, DMs from brands wanting to collaborate.

Jase watched in silent fury as every outlet picked up the story—none of them crediting him for the footage. His watermark had been effortlessly cropped out by reposts, and no one cared to ask who had actually captured the chaos.

He scrolled through Megan's Instagram, where she had just posted a solemn, heartfelt story about the dangers of fentanyl-laced substances and the importance of carrying Narcan. The post was flooded with praise.

"You're amazing."

"You literally saved a life. Wow."

"I'm buying Narcan today because of you."

Jase scoffed, his thumb hovering over the comment section. He wanted to type something—something biting, something that would reclaim his moment. But he knew it wouldn't matter. No one cared about the guy behind the camera. They never did.

Instead, he opened his own DMs. A few messages trickled in—some minor influencers asking for a collab, a couple of comments on his original video, but nothing close to the clout Megan was drowning in.

His stomach twisted with resentment.

She hadn't even tagged him.

He clenched his phone, jaw tightening. He had been cheated out of his own viral moment. And that? That wasn't something he was going to let slide.

CHAPTER 23:
COCO'S RUIN

Coco Rivera woke up in a sterile hospital room, her throat dry and her body weak. The harsh fluorescent lighting felt like knives behind her eyelids, her temples throbbing with the aftermath of whatever poison had nearly ended her life. A beeping heart monitor kept time with her slow, ragged breathing. The scratchy hospital gown felt like sandpaper against her skin, a stark contrast to the tight, glittering club dress she last remembered wearing.

Then, it hit her.

The lounge. The coke. The overdose.

The panic set in before she even moved.

She bolted upright, gasping—only for a sharp pain to claw at her ribs, forcing her back down. Her fingers fumbled for her phone, desperate to piece together what had happened while she was unconscious. But it wasn't on the side table. Her pulse quickened. No phone meant no control over the narrative.

Before she could call out, the door creaked open.

A nurse walked in, clipboard in hand, eyes filled with that detached pity reserved for overdose cases.

"Ms. Rivera," the nurse said, voice calm but firm. "You're stable, but you need to rest. You were extremely lucky—"

Coco didn't care. "Where's my phone?"

The nurse hesitated. "It's with your personal belongings. But before we discuss that, the doctor needs to—"

"I don't need a doctor," Coco snapped, voice hoarse. "I need my damn phone."

The nurse sighed, clearly used to this kind of reaction. "I'll have someone bring it after we check your vitals."

Coco barely heard the words. Her mind was spinning, anxiety clawing at her insides. If people saw her in this state—if they saw her at all—it meant the story had already gotten out.

And then, as if summoned by the devil himself, a soft vibration sounded from the nurse's pocket. The woman sighed, pulled out a phone—not Coco's—and checked the screen before meeting Coco's frantic gaze.

"You're trending."

A Pitfall

It was worse than she could have imagined.

By the time she finally got her phone, it was too late. Footage of her limp body slumped in the booth at the Sand Dollar Lounge was *everywhere*. The lurid details of her overdose were dissected across social media, turning her into the city's latest cautionary tale.

Someone had uploaded close-up footage of her unconscious body, her lips blue, her chest frighteningly still. The comments were a battlefield.

"Another party girl bites the dust."

"Where's that 'strong, independent woman 'energy now?"

"Lmao, bet she blames someone else for this too."

It wasn't just the trolls. The local news stations ran with the story, airing her overdose on a loop, slotting her between rising crime rates and fentanyl PSAs. Her name was dragged through morning talk shows, her past indulgences now a topic for debate.

And then came the final blow.

The exposure didn't just kill her credibility—it obliterated it.

Her pending sexual assault case against Kyler was now a joke.

News outlets dissected her history with drugs, scrutinized her credibility, replayed clips of her wild nights, her erratic social media rants, and the damning footage from the lounge. Defense attorneys pounced, declaring her an unreliable witness. Overnight, the case unraveled.

Her lawyer dropped her via an impersonal email, citing "irreconcilable differences" and "compromised integrity." Desperate, she scrambled for new representation.

One by one, they shut her down.

The final call, to a well-known female attorney who had previously championed women's rights cases, was the hardest to stomach.

"I'm sorry, Ms. Rivera," the woman said, tone cool. "Given your... background, the DA will dismantle you on the stand. I can't take your case."

Coco ended the call without another word, staring blankly at her cracked phone screen.

Her world was crumbling.

CHAPTER 24:
COLLATERAL DAMAGE

Meanwhile, across the city, someone else was simmering with resentment.

Kimber McFadden, Kyler's younger sister, watched Megan Davenport's viral rescue video with clenched fists. Every comment, every fawning reply, made her stomach turn.

"She's not some goddamn hero," Kimber muttered, pacing her bedroom. "She's just another fame-hungry bitch riding a moment."

Her friend on FaceTime gave her a tired look. "You sound jealous, Kim."

"I *am* jealous," Kimber snapped. "Kyler's name is still being dragged in the dirt, but Megan's out here getting sponsorship deals because she happened to have Narcan?"

Her friend sighed. "She saved someone's life."

Kimber's jaw tightened. "She saved a *junkie*."

But the words tasted bitter the moment they left her lips. She knew this wasn't about Coco. This was about her—not being the center of attention. Not being the one people were talking about. She had spent years overshadowed by Kyler's messes, always a footnote in his scandals. Now, Megan was the one soaking up the limelight, and Kimber hated it.

The Forgotten Cameraman

In a dimly lit apartment reeking of stale weed and energy drinks, Jase sat hunched over his phone, scrolling through thousands of reuploads of *his* video.

Except it wasn't *his* anymore.

Megan's face was plastered across every major outlet, every influencer's account, every stitched reaction video.

Hashtags flooded his feed: #NarcanHero, #MeganDavenport, #SavedALife.

Jase's name?

Nowhere.

His footage had been stolen, cropped, repurposed—*monetized*—and he wasn't seeing a single dime from it.

He gritted his teeth, fingers tightening around his phone. He'd filmed the whole damn thing. The raw, unfiltered chaos. Megan had just *reacted*. She had played the good Samaritan role at the right time, while *he* had captured history.

And yet, she was getting all the credit.

Jase exhaled sharply through his nose, flicking open a DM. His fingers hovered over the keyboard before he started typing.

Jase: *Yo, TMZ. I got exclusive behind-the-scenes footage of the Megan Davenport overdose rescue. Unfiltered. The full story. Interested?*

He hit send.

If Megan wanted to play hero, he'd make sure the world saw the full picture.

CHAPTER 25: LEGAL MANEUVERS

Kyler sat alone on the balcony of his high-rise suite, a cigarette dangling between his fingers, glowing faintly against the neon-soaked skyline of Las Vegas. The city pulsed below him—cars weaving through the streets, billboards flashing promises of indulgence, and people moving in a blur of vice and desperation.

He exhaled slowly, watching the smoke curl into the night air, his phone pressed to his ear.

Brayden's voice crackled through the speaker, brimming with satisfaction.

Brayden (through the phone):" We have a golden opportunity here, Ky. With Coco's overdose plastered everywhere, her credibility is fucking torched. The DA is gonna have to reconsider everything."

Kyler's lips curled slightly—not quite a smile, but the shadow of one. It wasn't relief, not exactly. More like the moment when a losing hand suddenly turns to a full house.

Kyler (exhaling, measured):" About time I caught a break."

The weight of the past few months sat heavy on him—court hearings, media scrutiny, whispers behind his back. The accusations had stuck to him like tar, impossible to scrub clean, and now, like some cosmic joke, the one person who could bury him had imploded in front of the world.

His gaze drifted toward the strip, the flashing lights reflected in his dark irises. He knew the game wasn't over yet, but the tide had turned.

Then, a thought slithered into his mind, coiling around his conscience like smoke. If the fentanyl-laced cocaine had finished the job, he wouldn't have to deal with Coco at all. The problem would have erased itself. No trial, no he-said-she-said courtroom spectacle. Just silence.

He took another drag from his cigarette, the ember flaring bright.

Kyler (low, almost to himself):" She was inches away."

Brayden:" Yeah, but she made it. For now."

The words hung between them, heavy with implication.

Brayden (more serious):" Look, don't do anything reckless. Let me handle it. This isn't the time to lose your head."

Kyler's jaw tensed. He wasn't stupid—he knew the walls had ears, that every move he made was being watched. But the temptation was there, gnawing at the edges of his mind.

He tapped the ash from his cigarette, his fingers steady.

Kyler (calm, calculated):" Do what you have to do."

A pause. Then, Brayden chuckled.

Brayden:" That's what I like to hear."

The call ended with a soft click.

Kyler leaned back in his chair, letting the city lights wash over him. The game had just changed. Now, it was time to make his next move.

CHAPTER 26: ALL IS TWISTED THAT ENDS TWISTED

Coco Rivera had spent years crafting an image of effortless luxury. Every nightclub appearance, every designer outfit, every candid photo leaked to the internet tabloids was carefully curated to solidify her status as the reigning queen of the Strip. She wasn't just another Vegas socialite—she was an *institution*. Her name for a time opened doors, her presence turned heads, and her phone held the keys to an empire built on connections and indulgence.

Until one night shattered it all.

The overdose became the only thing people saw when they looked at her now. No one cared about who she knew or who she was dating or the elite afterparties she once dominated. The photos of her slumped in a booth at the Sand Dollar Lounge, skin pale and lips blue, were burned into the city's consciousness. She wasn't Coco Rivera anymore. She was a *cautionary tale*.

Her phone, once buzzing with endless messages—club promoters, brand deals, friends begging for invites—had gone eerily silent. Calls went straight to voicemail. Her social media engagement plummeted overnight. The high rollers saw her coming in the casinos now and avoided her like a sinking ship.

Desperation clawed at her as she pressed a trembling hand to her temple, pacing her penthouse. She had spent years at the top. She couldn't disappear *now*.

She called her attorney.

"Please, I—I need representation," she stammered, voice hoarse from days of stress and withdrawal. "You *know* the truth. You *know* what happened to me—"

"Ms. Rivera," her lawyer interrupted coolly. "Given the circumstances and your... background, I don't see a way forward. The DA will tear you apart on the stand."

Silence. The finality in the woman's tone cut through her like a knife.

Click.

Coco stared at her phone in disbelief. The silence around her felt suffocating. The city moved on so quickly. And for the first time, she was truly alone.

Megan Davenport had never wanted to be famous *this* way.

When she stepped in that night and saved Coco's life, it hadn't been for the cameras. It was instinct. She had carried Narcan ever since losing a friend to an overdose two prior. She never thought she'd actually *use* it. And yet, here she was.

Viral.

Her face was plastered across every Vegas news outlet, her name trending for days. *Las Vegas Influencer Saves Overdose Victim— A Real-Life Hero!* Journalists flooded her inbox, morning shows invited her for interviews, brands wanted to slap their logo onto her newfound fame.

Her fingers hesitated over the DM requests.

Hey, we'd love to partner with you as an ambassador for overdose awareness—

She swiped away, overwhelmed. Thousands of comments flooded her latest post:

"You're amazing! An angel in human form!"

"This is why we need more people like Megan!!"

"She's literally saving lives, and y'all wanna talk about her being an influencer?"

And then there were the skeptics:

"She had Narcan on her? Kinda sus, don't you think?"

"Megan's just another clout chaser. Would she have saved Coco if no cameras were around?"

She squeezed her phone, her heart pounding. The praise, the backlash—it was too much. One moment of doing the right thing, and suddenly, the internet had decided she was a *story*. A hero. A fraud. A savior. A liar.

She hadn't asked for any of it. But now? Now, there was no going back.

Jase sat in his apartment, scrolling through his feed with a scowl.

His footage had been *everywhere*. He had been the one to film the overdose, the frantic rescue, the gasps of the crowd as Coco clung to life. It was *his* video that had blown up first.

But who was getting all the attention?

Megan.

Jase clenched his jaw. He had been *there first*. He had *captured* it. And now? His name was a footnote. The media latched onto Megan's face, her act of heroism, her perfectly tearful soundbites.

And what did Jase get?

Nothing.

He pulled up the original video, watching it again, bile rising in his throat. His numbers had spiked, sure—but *not like hers*. She was on morning talk shows. She was landing sponsorships. And him? Just another guy behind the camera.

He flicked his cigarette into the ashtray, exhaling sharply.

"Unbelievable."

Kimber McFadden wanted to scream.

She stared at her phone, scrolling through the endless news articles and glowing headlines about her #1 covert competition. *Megan the Hero. Megan the Savior. Megan this, Megan that.*

Kimber had spent *years* grinding in the influencer world, clawing her way to relevance. And now? Megan was being *handed* everything.

"Everyone's acting like she's some saint," Kimber muttered to her friend over brunch, stabbing at her overpriced avocado toast. "She's just another attention-hungry influencer."

Her friend barely looked up, too engrossed in another video of Megan's TV interview.

Kimber's stomach twisted. She had spent her whole life in Kyler's shadow—his chaos, his scandals, his notorious notoriety always eclipsing whatever she did. And now, when *he* finally faded into the background, Megan stepped into the spotlight instead.

It wasn't fair. It wasn't *right*.

And yet, deep down, she knew it didn't matter. Megan had the story now.

And Kimber was just *another extra.*

Kyler lit a cigarette, exhaling as he leaned against the balcony railing of his penthouse. Below him, Vegas pulsed with life—drunken tourists, flashing billboards, the neon heartbeat of the Strip.

Brayden's voice crackled through the phone.

"We have a golden opportunity here, Ky. Coco's credibility is *fucking* torched. The DA's case is crumbling."

Kyler smirked, tapping ash into the night air.

"Poor Coco," he drawled. "What a tragedy."

Brayden chuckled. "The defense is gonna rip her apart. We keep the pressure up, and you walk."

Kyler took another drag, exhaling slowly. Coco had been *dangerous* —too close to bringing him down. But now? She was a joke. She wasn't testifying against *anyone.*

If she had *died,* this would've been even easier.

He let the thought hang in the air before pushing it away.

"Do what you have to do," he said smoothly.

Brayden's laugh was dark. "That's what I like to hear."

The call ended. Kyler crushed the cigarette beneath his heel, watching the embers scatter.

In Vegas, the strong didn't just *survive.*

They *thrived.*

CHAPTER 27: PARKING LOT JUSTICE

The neon glow of Dino's Dive Bar sign flickered weakly in the haze of cigarette smoke and dry desert air. The parking lot was a patchwork of cracked asphalt and oil stains, a haven for late-night scuffles and petty dramas. Jase leaned casually against his 1969 Ford Mustang, the yellow-and-black paint gleaming under the streetlights. The car was parked diagonally across two spaces, its stance as arrogant as its owner.

The night had a restless energy, the kind that came with too much booze, too many grudges, and a city that never truly slept. Kyler emerged from the bar with his sister Kimber and two new friends, their laughter cutting through the stagnant air. He was riding high, the weight of his legal troubles suddenly lifted. The charges had been dropped, and he was free—at least for now. His Harley-Davidson sat gleaming nearby, a rebellious contrast to the Mustang's polished bravado.

Kyler's eyes flicked over Jase's car, his lips curling in disdain. "Who the hell parks like that?" he muttered, shaking his head. Kimber rolled her eyes, already sensing trouble brewing.

Jase straightened, smirking as he took a drag from his cigarette. "Hey, lowlife," he called out, his voice cutting through the parking lot. "Enjoying your freedom? Must feel nice to slip through the cracks of justice."

Kyler froze, his grip tightening on his handlebars. He turned slowly, his eyes narrowing. "You should learn how to park."

Kimber grabbed his arm, her tone urgent. "Ignore him. Let's go."

Jase snorted, flicking his cigarette butt onto the ground. "That's right. Listen to your OnlyFans whore of a sister. Always knew she'd be good for something."

The air in the parking lot went still, tension coiling like a spring. Kimber's face darkened, but she pulled Kyler toward his bike. "He's not worth it," she hissed.

Kyler climbed onto his Harley, revving the engine loudly enough to drown out his rage. Kimber and the others piled into a beat-up sedan, and they began to pull out of the lot. But Kyler wasn't letting it go. He followed them down the street until they stopped at a red light. Then, with a sharp turn, he circled back toward Dino's.

Jase was still lounging by his car, scrolling on his phone, utterly unaware of what was coming. Kyler crept up from behind, his wallet chain in hand. The soft clink of metal was the only warning before he looped it around Jase's neck and yanked.

Jase gasped, his phone clattering to the ground. Kyler's voice was low, venomous. "You still wanna talk shit? Talk shit now."

The chain tightened as Jase clawed at his neck, his face turning crimson. Kyler kicked the back of his knee, sending him to the ground. The Mustang's polished bumper gleamed like a silent witness to the violence.

"Get off!" Jase choked, his voice rasping as he struggled to breathe. Desperation kicked in, and he twisted his leg around Kyler's, using the leverage to flip him over his hip. Kyler hit the asphalt with a grunt, momentarily winded.

Jase scrambled up, rage blazing in his eyes. When Kyler lunged with a kick aimed squarely at his groin, Jase sidestepped and caught his leg, dragging him down to the ground. He pinned Kyler and unleashed a flurry of punches, his knuckles splitting as they connected with Kyler's face.

"Enough!" Kimber's voice rang out, sharp and commanding. Before Jase could react, a burst of electricity surged through him as Kimber drove her taser into the back of his neck. Jase crumpled, convulsing on the ground as Kimber stood over him, her chest heaving.

"You dumb motherfucker," she spat, crouching to pull Jase's wallet from his back pocket. She rifled through it, taking the cash before tossing it onto his chest. "You shouldn't have been talking shit."

She turned to her brother, who was groaning and wiping blood from his face. "Come on," she said, helping him to his feet. Kyler pulled a small vial of coke from his jacket, taking a quick bump to clear his head. His nostrils flared, and his eyes sharpened as the rush hit him.

"Let's get out of here," Kyler muttered, climbing back onto his bike. Kimber slid into the car with the others, and they peeled out of the lot just as the wail of sirens cut through the night.

Jase lay sprawled on the ground, groaning as the police cruisers pulled into the lot. The Mustang's black-and-yellow paint seemed almost mocking under the flashing blue lights. Kimber and Kyler were already disappearing down Las Vegas Boulevard, leaving Jase to face the consequences of his big mouth and bad parking.

CHAPTER 28: VERONICA REGARDING THE PHOTOGRAPHER

After the chaos of Tiffany and Westin skipping town and Coco's reluctant return to the suffocating grip of her gambling-addict father and alcoholic stepmother, life in Vegas slithered back to its usual rhythm—an endless cycle of neon-drenched nights and desperate hustles. The house Coco returned to was steeped in a permanent haze of cigarette smoke, the walls yellowed by years of bad decisions. The furniture reeked of stale beer and broken dreams, the kind of place where time stood still, and hope had long since packed its bags.

Meanwhile, Elizabeth and Veronica kept the game running at the Sand Dollar Lounge, their presence a seamless blend of temptation and transaction. They moved like seasoned performers in a cabaret of vice, flirting with wide-eyed tourists and seasoned regulars alike, their charm a well-oiled machine designed to keep the money flowing. But Veronica had a problem—her OnlyFans content had gone stagnant. She needed fresh material, and more importantly, she needed a new male talent.

Slim Mo, her previous go-to, had become a liability. He let his own vices dictate his priorities, and the balance had shifted—he was no longer working for her, but for himself. He started demanding a cut she wasn't willing to give, and worse, he had stopped being easily finessed. The moment a man stopped seeing the privilege of being in her presence as its own form of currency, he became useless. So, she cut him off.

That left her with a dilemma: she needed a new photographer, someone who could deliver high-quality images and, if she played her cards right, someone she could mold to her advantage.

She drafted a Craigslist ad with the precision of a seasoned con artist baiting a mark.

"Boudoir Photographer Wanted for Bi-Weekly Shoots."

Short. Professional. Just enough to pique the right kind of interest without raising red flags. She knew exactly the type of men who would respond—bored hobbyists, desperate wannabes, and, if she was lucky, someone with real talent who could be nudged, teased, and manipulated into giving her exactly what she needed.

Now, it was a waiting game.

The response came quickly.

An email landed in her inbox late that night:
"I am an art & boudoir photographer. I live & work downtown. Here is a link to my portfolio. Boudoir shoots start at $800. If you want to stop by tomorrow, we can take some test shots and discuss working together."

The next day, Veronica stood in the doorway of his studio, the scent of cedar wood and nag champa incense wrapping around her like an invitation. She tilted her head slightly, taking in the photographer who had answered her call—a tall, lean man with dark hair and sharp features, his arms defined beneath the snug fit of his black T-shirt. His presence was quiet, controlled, the kind of man who let his work speak for itself.

"Hi, I'm the one from Craigslist," she said, her voice smooth like honey laced with something just a little dangerous.

"Come in," he said, stepping aside. His gaze flicked over her in a way that was more professional than predatory, but there was no missing the shift in his posture—the way he squared his shoulders, the way his breath caught for just a fraction of a second.

Veronica stepped inside, her boots clicking against the polished concrete floor. She was a vision of effortless sensuality—denim cutoffs that hugged her hips like a second skin, a sheer, nearly see-through tee that clung to her curves in all the right places. A Prada men's Saffiano-leather tote was slung casually over her shoulder, the contradiction of high-end luxury and rugged allure making her even more intoxicating. Her long black mane of hair cascaded to her waist, glossy and untamed, framing the hazel warmth of her eyes.

He closed the door behind her, watching as she walked further in, her scent—a mix of vanilla, cinnamon gum, and something uniquely her—lingering in the air.

"Are these for your partner?" he asked, already anticipating the answer but wanting to hear it from her lips.

Veronica smirked, stepping closer, her gaze playful yet razor-sharp. "No," she purred. "I need images and video for my OnlyFans."

He arched a brow, crossing his arms. "What's your vision?"

"I need fresh content every two weeks—three different looks per shoot, and I need video."

He studied her for a moment, considering. "I don't shoot video."

She tilted her head, eyes dancing with mischief. "You can hold a phone, can't you?"

A slow smirk spread across his lips. "I can. But that's extra. On top of my base rate."

She stepped even closer now, standing just inside his personal space, the cinnamon on her breath intoxicating. "And your base rate is...?"

"$800 for the photos, $400 for ten minutes of iPhone video," he said, his voice steady despite the heat between them. "I'm not editing the video."

Veronica let her gaze drift down his frame, taking her time before locking eyes with him again. "Deal. How about we get started now?"

The air between them was thick with an unspoken challenge, a collision of professionalism and something much more primal. The photographer's eyes lingered just a second too long before he turned his attention back to the set, adjusting the lighting with the practiced ease of a man who had done this countless times before—though something about this session already felt different.

Veronica smirked, sensing the shift. She let the moment hang, unzipping her tote bag with deliberate slowness before shrugging it off entirely. With a lazy stretch, she raised her arms above her head, knowing full well what it did to the sheer fabric of her worn-in tee. It rode up just enough to reveal a sliver of golden skin, the smooth lines of her stomach catching the soft glow of the studio lights. The heat in the room changed—subtle, but unmistakable.

She took a step forward, closing some of the distance between them, the faint scent of cinnamon gum and expensive perfume lingering in the air. His hands paused on the light stand. A slight hitch in his breath—almost imperceptible, but not to someone like her.

"This is going to be fun," she murmured, her lips curving into something between a challenge and an invitation.

The photographer swallowed, resetting his stance, forcing himself to focus. "Let's get started," he said, his voice even, but she caught the edge in it.

Veronica smiled to herself as she stepped onto the set.

This was going to be one hell of a session.

CHAPTER 29: YOU'VE BEEN TO BALI?

She ran her fingers along the outside of his pants, feigning interest in a poster on the wall. Her touch was light, teasing, her nails barely grazing the thick ridge pressing against the fabric. He inhaled sharply but didn't pull away. Instead, he let her play, watching her with hooded eyes, dark with intent. The air between them felt charged, like static before a storm.

"Is that poster an original?" she asked, her voice barely above a whisper.

He nodded, stepping closer, so close she could feel the heat of his body against hers. His breath, hot and sweet, ghosted over her lips. She twirled a lock of hair between her fingers, gaze locked onto his, playful, daring. He moved in, brushing a strand behind her ear, his fingers lingering, tracing the shell. Her skin prickled under his touch, a delicious shiver running down her spine.

She let her other hand drift lower, fingers dancing along his belt. "Where'd you get that one?" she murmured, gesturing at another framed print, though neither of them gave a damn about the art.

"A flea market in Bali."

Her breath hitched. "Bali? I've never been."

He smirked, a lazy, knowing grin. "I could take you."

The way he said it sent a pulse between her legs. A promise. An invitation. She inched closer, her ample breasts brushing against his chest, and felt the solid, undeniable proof of his arousal pressing into her hip. Her lips parted. His eyes flicked down to them. The tension between them snapped like a tightrope giving way.

He grabbed Veronicas waist and yanked her flush against him. Their lips met in a fervent clash of need—wet, demanding, tongues tangling, tasting. She moaned into his mouth, fingers tightening around his belt, nails scraping along the leather as she tugged it free. He groaned, hands palming her ass, squeezing, pulling her even closer.

Her tiny top was gone in an instant, yanked over her head and discarded. He drank her in, eyes devouring the way her olive skin glowed under the dim lights, nipples hard and eager for his touch. He bent his head, lips wrapping around one, tongue flicking, circling, sucking. Her back arched, a gasp spilling from her lips.

"My nipples are so sensitive," she whispered, voice ragged. He responded by pinching one and sucking harder on the other, sending jolts of pleasure straight to her core.

As he worshipped her breasts, she undid his jeans, her fingers trembling with anticipation. She pressed her palm against the thick length still trapped in his briefs, feeling the heat of him, the twitch of need. "I wanna travel too," she breathed, dragging her fingers along his waistband.

"You will, baby," he murmured, voice thick, husky, filled with promises of more. He kissed down her stomach, knelt before her, and slid her pants off in one swift motion. Her panties were soaked, a damp spot marking where she needed him most.

He ran his fingers along the outside of her drenched lace, teasing, taunting. She squirmed. He inhaled deeply, exhaling warm breath against her wet heat. When he finally peeled them off, his tongue was on her instantly, a slow, torturous glide that made her whimper. Her fingers tangled in his hair, tugging him closer, guiding his mouth where she needed it most.

She could feel herself unraveling, could feel the heat building, coiling tight in her belly. His hands gripped her thighs, keeping her spread open as he licked and sucked, his tongue dipping inside her, his nose pressed against her, inhaling her scent like he was addicted.

"I really wanna see him," she moaned, voice trembling as his fingers tapped against her slick entrance.

He rose to his feet, and she dropped to her knees before him. Looking up through thick lashes, her lips parted as she rubbed her palms over his thick, swollen length. When she freed him from his briefs, his cock sprang out, thick, heavy, slapping against her chin. She gripped the base, holding it against her cheek, marveling at its size.

"You're so big," she whispered, smearing the pre-cum across her lips, tasting him.

She spit into her hands, slicking his shaft with slow, deliberate strokes, teasing before finally taking him into her mouth. The first inch, then another, until she felt him press against the back of her throat. She gagged slightly, saliva dripping down her chin. She loved the way he groaned, the way he tangled his fingers in her hair, the way his thighs tensed as she worked him over.

"I'm ready to see Bali," she murmured, voice dripping with desire.

Afterward, they lay tangled together, skin slick with sweat, breaths slowing. The scent of sex lingered, heavy and intoxicating.

He traced lazy circles on her back. "So, how did you decide on shooting with me, Veronica?"

She turned her head to him, still catching her breath. "I checked out your work on Instagram. I saw you shot for Kimber McFadden and Megan Davenport. They tagged you as the photographer on their grids." She ran a finger over his chest. "How do you know them?"

He hesitated, just for a second. "My older brother knows them."

She stilled. A strange prickle ran down her spine.

"Your older brother?" she repeated slowly, propping herself up on an elbow.

He nodded, watching her, unaware of the growing tension in her body. "Yeah."

A cold knot formed in her stomach. The room suddenly felt smaller, the air too thick, too warm.

"Who's your older brother?" Her voice came out quieter than she intended, almost like she already knew the answer but didn't want to hear it.

He glanced at her, casually, oblivious. "His name's Bradford."

Everything inside her turned to ice.

She sat up fully, sheets pooling at her waist. Her heartbeat pounded in her ears. "Bradford Atreydese?" she demanded, eyes wide, breath shallow.

"Yeah," he said, like it was nothing, like he hadn't just detonated a bomb inside her chest.

She stared at him, mouth slightly open, mind racing, replaying everything, every touch, every kiss, every filthy thing they had just done.

Oh. My. God.

Fuck me.

She had just made content—on camera—for her OnlyFans page—with **Bradford Atreydese's younger brother.**

Las Vegas was a small town, but **this** was insane.

Her stomach flipped. A heat that had nothing to do with lust spread through her body. Panic. Shock. A sudden, overwhelming sense of **what the fuck have I done?**

She needed a drink. Or maybe she needed to throw up.

He was watching her now, a curious tilt to his head. "What's wrong?"

She forced out a laugh—thin, nervous, barely holding it together. "Nothing," she lied. "It's just… fuck. This town is **way** too small."

Chloe at the department store

Kvler McFadden

Jase

Tammie & Tiff

Veronica